THE KING WILL

MAKE A WAY

A STORY FOR THE

LAST DAYS SAINT

Lee Giles

ISBN 1456339311

For the King

THE KING WILL MAKE A WAY

Chapter 1

"We'll tell them the King is dead."

"But the people will still remember him."

"We'll make them forget, simply stop mentioning him. He won't exist to the children. He just stays up there on that hill of his, never to be seen. It will be easy."

The discussion was one of hushed excitement, rather than heated debate. Vulpine, the elected leader of the village assembly and the self-appointed leader of the Brothers and Sons, answered everyone's qualms. He spoke with such certitude that those around him often quickly acquiesced, though he considered it a bother to always have to explain himself. Tall and dark, he used his size to stare down his competitors and used his quick mind to silence them. His piercing eyes appeared black against the contrasting whites, which lent to the aura of the man.

"Good doctor, would you be obliged to help us in the matter?" Vulpine turned everyone's attention toward the village physician.

"You mean something along the lines of...." the good doctor cleared his throat, "Upon examination, it is my conclusion that the King died peacefully in his sleep from nothing other than ripe old age." He practiced the diagnosis in his most professional voice.

"Something along those lines would do splendidly," Vulpine said smirking and suggested a drink.

"Gabe!" he bellowed, pausing the clandestine meeting. "Why does a guest have to holler for a drink?" he growled toward the kitchen.

Gabe, a small boy for ten, came out cautiously with a tray of drinks, taking one step at a time as if checking to make sure the floorboards were solid before putting his weight down. The windowless kitchen door swung back and forth behind him while he made his way across the wooden floor without a misstep, even though his golden hair threatened to block his view and cause a catastrophe. He relieved himself of his load, transferring the burden to the heavy oak table. Gabe made an about-face as if under a general's orders and headed straight back to the kitchen.

Behind closed doors, he asked his mother again why Father let those men use their family's inn for meetings.

2

"I've answered you already" was all she responded, without taking her eyes off the pie crust she was rolling out. She was always at work, an ant in an apron. This is where Gabe saw her most often, in the kitchen. The room showed signs of her handiwork: the drying herbs hanging from the rafters, the pot of stew bubbling on the hearth, and, of course, the round pie dough growing ever thinner. Gabe watched her pause to brush brown wisps of hair from her face. People often teased her that her food must not be any good since she was so slender, but she never took offense because it was widely known no one could bake a pie or season a stew like Mother. Wiping the flour off her hands, she looked at Gabe, who seemed to be hanging there as if out to dry. She sighed and smiled. "Why don't you ask your father?" she suggested and set back to work.

Gabe knew just where to find his father in the evenings, and from the kitchen he climbed the creaky stairs that led to the bed chambers. The largest was their family quarters. There were two beds in it—as long as the inn wasn't crowded and an extra bed wasn't needed elsewhere. The room also held Father's small table and chair. Here he sat with the inn's books, recording the day's accounts, meticulously adding and subtracting, keeping the inn prospering, if modestly.

Gabe was often told he looked like his father, but Gabe didn't believe that. Apart from their shared heritage of golden hair and green eyes with flecks of brown, Gabe didn't think it was possible that he could grow into his father's image.

"Father?" Gabe's father turned his head to see his son standing inside the door. Father straightened and warmly welcomed Gabe to his side. Gabe repeated the question he had just asked Mother.

"Because I love you," his father began, "and because I love your mother and your sisters. I want to take care of you all the best I can. I know you aren't used to serving in the dining hall, but they want you to be the only one to come into the room during their meetings. Gabe, they are paying customers. The inn is mostly empty now that it is fall. You understand, right?" Gabe nodded. With a smile and a pat, his father turned back to his books under the flicker of the candle flame.

Gabe flopped down the stairs and, seeing he wasn't in demand in the kitchen, he slipped out of the inn into the cool night air. He knew he might be needed inside, but he made a roaming retreat back to the kitchen, circling first around the inn. Shuffling his feet, he paused to look at the well-weathered sign in front of their two-story inn. It simply read, "There Is Always Room."

There was plenty of room now that traveling season was over and fall had arrived. Gabe wondered if there was another way he could help make money for the family so those brusque men wouldn't have to be welcomed anymore. Gabe leaned against the wooden frame of the inn and looked at the hill, which was their nearest neighbor to the east. He stood there wondering how one went about finding work and shrunk back as he realized he'd have to ask someone if they needed a boy. He imagined himself frozen in front of someone's stables while a man stood before him demanding to know why he'd come. He pictured his mouth ajar, the words caught in his throat. *A croakless toad, that's what I am. Why is it so hard to spit out that first word?* He shook his head as if to knock the thoughts out of his mind, wanting to leave them out there in the dirt to be trampled on, and entered through the side door back to safety at his mother's side.

Waiting for his next order, Gabe leaned against the wall just next to the double-hinged door in order to hear the men. This was hardly necessary for though the men spoke mostly in faint tones, they were quick to raise the rafters with their shouts for him. As he rested against the wall, soaking in the scent of freshly grated cinnamon, he heard one voice above the others. What he heard made his eyes stretch wide and his mouth pop open as if his chin had just dropped anchor.

"The King is dead!" Vulpine raised his glass in a toast, and the phrase echoed around the plain wooden room.

****

The King sat in his resplendent hilltop abode, very much alive. King's Hill, as it was known, lay on the village's eastern boundary. No one ever set foot on it. For as long as anyone in his family remembered, there had always been a guard on duty at the foot of the hill, and everyone grew up knowing King's Hill was off limits to the villagers.

Although not by any means an imposing mountain, its name did stretch its definition, and it towered over the village. One side of the hill was always dressed in forest green, ranks of conifers acting as a shield between the King and the village. Luscious green covered the base where the pines didn't conceal it from the sun, and the meadow grass always danced in the breeze which rolled down the hill like a giggling child. Wild flowers, violet and gold, stood in defiance of the falling temperatures. The trees which filled out the rest of the hill embraced the cool air and were as golden as the sun reflecting off the King's crown.

Approaching the pinnacle, the greens and golds gave way to gray as the hill became solid rock at its summit. It was there at the peak the King's home had been hewn from the side of the hill. In the center of this stony alcove, inlaid with gold, stood the throne. Over the throne a white banner hung, waving its message of the King's love for the village.

Under the banner the King sat, watching over the village, always knowing everything that happened. He knew exactly what had been said at the meeting and hadn't been surprised—he was never surprised by anything.

It was there in his throne room at the top of the village that the King listened to his song, which the trees and streams and flowers and even the rocks sang toward his throne continuously. Vulpine had decided it would be sung in the village only once more—at the King's funeral.

****

Vulpine's right-hand man, Phineas Tract, was more than an assistant; he acted as Vulpine's mouthpiece to the public. Vulpine spoke to Phineas and Phineas parroted the words to the villagers. He lacked in hair as much as he lacked in height, and he was a good foot shorter than his master. Though not a slave, he was certainly obedient to Vulpine. His gift lay not in an appealing appearance but in his smooth voice that calmed jittery crowds. The friendly, reassuring voice he used when explaining things made people feel as if everything were under control, even if they didn't understand what he was saying.

To talk with the villagers, he would stroll down to the square, which was the center of village life. People

7

congregated around the well in the middle of the square to hear the latest gossip, or they walked along the shops which walled in the square on two sides. There was the tailor, butcher, shoemaker, doctor and candy man. There was also the metalsmith, who could make metal pour, and the glass blower, who could make glass bend.

While some shops sold cloth, tools and other household wares, there was also a daily market that began where the square ended. The only dividing marker was a bell tower, which held the copper bell that beckoned the villagers to the square for important events and announcements. Beyond the tower were brightly painted wooden stalls full of every kind of sight and scent: pies, licorice, rum, pickles, birds, canes, toys, rugs. Any villager in need of something could find it in the market or at least someone willing to make it for them, at a price.

Children would beg a peppermint stick and then run ahead, weaving through the shoppers to play in the lake which formed the western boundary of the village. Each evening the sun dipped into the lake, setting it on fire. The village children, however, didn't come for its beauty. They liked the cool tickle on their toes as they dangled their feet in the water, sending ripples gliding over its surface. Later, the children returned home heading in every direction, leaving muddy footprints along the roads which lead out of each corner of the square, some passing the school where the wealthier families sent their children to study.

It seemed as if everyone visited the square at least once every day, and Phineas was no exception. Almost every day he sauntered into the open area like the Pied Piper, and curious villagers would follow him. They trooped together to the east end of the Square where the impressive government building, the Assembly Hall, stood, its pillars proclaiming its importance. Phineas would climb the steps that lined the front of the Hall, as it was commonly known and, positioning himself on its porch, he would deliver the daily digest.

The day the King's death was announced was no different. Phineas reported how the King had died peacefully in his sleep and announced his funeral would take place the following day. Step by step, everything had been carefully orchestrated—by Vulpine.

Chapter 2

No one worked on the day of the funeral. Fog misted over the village as the King's song was sung by his grave. After the ceremony, Gabe plodded home with his family, thinking through all he knew about the King. He knew the King had founded the village about a hundred years before and set as its foundation, a book of laws he had written himself. He didn't know anything about the book or its laws and nor could he think of anything else he knew about the King.

Back at home, Gabe's family sat around the table together. They lived at the inn but ate in the kitchen, the large room being reserved for guests only. Eating a cold meal and discussing the King, Gabe inundated his parents with questions.

Gabe's two sisters, who sat side by side holding hands under the table, were listening. The older one could have been Gabe's identical twin if she hadn't been born a girl. Not only did both have Father's golden hair, but also his eyes.

Whenever they asked their father what color their eyes were, he'd say, "The color of muddy grass."

Five-year-old Tabitha, with her brown curls and equally dark wide eyes, adored everything about her big sister and stuck to her like the freckles on her nose. Living up to her angelic name, Angela never seemed bothered by her little sidekick. She patiently explained to her why cows needed milking and why the sun went to sleep every night. Though just ten like Gabe, Angela always seemed to know the answer to anything. Now she seemed content just to listen.

"Did you ever see the King?" Gabe wanted to know. "Why didn't the King ever come down? Why didn't he ever talk to us?"

Gabe's father was a wise and humble man, slow to speak and slow to anger. He took Gabe's questions seriously and pondered on each a bit before answering.

"I never did get a chance to see the King, but I know that he used to visit the villagers. My grandfather used to talk about it. He was just a young boy at the time. He said the King was a majestic sight, wearing a golden crown and his royal robe. My grandfather said everyone flocked to be near him because he was full of wisdom and grace.

"No one is quite sure what happened to make the King leave or why he never returned. But my father once told me that he suspected the leaders of our village one day asked him not to return. He thought they were jealous the people adored the King and hung on his words and not theirs. The King left peacefully. At least that's what my father told me.

"People have different ideas about it all, but one thing is sure. When the King left, he told the villagers he would see them again. He said that he hoped it would be a pleasant encounter, but he feared many would not welcome his return."

"But he never did return, right, Father?"

"No, he never did."

"Why would the King say he would come back and not keep his word?" The question had pestered Gabe for days. He and Angela, with Tabitha in her shadow, were lugging water from the family's well out back to Betty, their milk cow.

"He didn't know he was going to die, Gabe. He just didn't get back in time. He wasn't trying to break his word. It just happened." Angela thought it was a reasonable explanation.

"I don't know. If he really just slipped away in his sleep, he must have known he was getting close to the end of his life. Why wouldn't he keep his promise before he died?" Gabe was more airing his thoughts than searching for answers from his sister. "If he was as wonderful as some people think, he would have come back before he died."

"Why is this bothering you?" Angela didn't understand what Gabe was feeling. "So he didn't come back. What's the big deal? We lived without him. Our parents have lived without him. Things are okay. We didn't need him to come back. He never did anything. We're okay without him."

Gabe wasn't feeling okay but he kept quiet. Morning chores were soon finished and the children joined their parents at the table for breakfast. After warm bowls of sloppy mush, or at least as Gabe was eating his, Father produced an intricately carved wooden box and laid it carefully on the table. "What is it, Father?" Tabitha asked, wiggling with impatience.

"This box was my grandfather's. Then it was my father's. Then it was mine."

"What's inside of it?" Tabitha pressed, not satisfied with his answer.

Father smiled and leaned back a bit. "After our discussion about the King, I remembered this old box. I admit it has just sat neglected, stashed away for years. I guess I put it away to keep it from damage since it was so old and beautiful. But in putting it aside, I forgot about it. I spent the last few days trying to find it."

Tabitha didn't understand why Father was telling them about the box he had put away so well he had forgotten all about it. And she couldn't understand why the box was remembered and on the table now. "But what is it, Father?" she couldn't help but ask again.

Without a word, he opened the box. It was full of old papers, yellowed and wrinkled with age. Father laughed at Tabitha, who looked as if she expected a new doll to be buried under the stack.

This time Angela spoke up. "Are they old letters? Maybe great-grandfather's love letters to his wife." Angela was pleased with the thought.

"No, Angela, but they are written by my grandfather; at least, written in his hand. It's a copy of the King's law. Today, the law book is just considered an historical book. You know it's kept locked in a glass case in the Assembly Hall. But years ago, it was the law of the village, and my grandfather used to go with his family to hear the King's law read aloud daily in the Hall. His father must have had him write down what he heard as part of his education."

Gabe's interest was piqued, and he moved to the edge of his seat. He was sure that this would make all the uncertainty go away. Gabe's father had been watching his reaction and speaking to Gabe, he said, "And as part of your education, today you may be excused to read through all these papers." In a flash, Gabe gathered up the box and raced out to the animal shed to be alone with his great-grandfather's work, the King's words.

Vulpine was sure no one knew any of the King's words anymore and moved to erase from the village all memory of the King. The Brothers and Sons had met and decided to hold a competition to distract the villagers from the King's funeral and to get rid of what current ties to the King—his banner and his song. Phineas announced that in just two weeks, the winning banner and song would be revealed to the public.

The village artisans got right to work, and the village filled with excited chatter over the competitors' creations. The only rule they worked under was this: the banner or song had to be completely new and different in order to lead the village into the future.

Gabe, however, wasn't thinking about the competition; his thoughts were always on the King. He was keen to report what he had learned from reading the King's law and felt confirmed in his suspicion that something was amiss. He was literally bouncing in his seat, waiting for his family to settle in for the evening meal.

As soon as he had the chance, he poured out all that he had bottled up. "He said in the book of law that he would come back. It's in there! It also says that all the words of the law are sure and true, that the King's word cannot fail. He couldn't have died without coming back to the village!" Gabe spilled his words, his mouth trying to keep pace with his mind.

15

"I still don't see how that matters." Angela didn't find Gabe's excitement contagious. "He died. He couldn't help it that he died before he came back."

Gabe deflated and looked to his father. "Gabe," Father began, "thanks for reading through those for us. I'm sure there are some other interesting things you could share with us." Gabe nodded and abandoned his attempt to convince them that the King had to still be alive. He told them other tidbits of the law but didn't stop believing the King was still living on the hill.

Two weeks passed quickly. As Gabe read and reread the King's law, artists brought their banners and presented them to the Assembly, the men elected to lead the village. Vulpine easily swayed the majority to his opinion. With mere comments, he led the Assemblymen to choose the banner that would serve his plans best.

The new banner was green to symbolize the fertile farm lands that ran the length of the road between the inn and the square and stretched back more than half a mile from the farm houses on each side. On the wide end of the banner was a depiction of the Assembly Hall, honoring its preeminence in the village. The banner came to a point where there was a picture of the well, symbolizing life. Vulpine approved the banner's meaning: the Assembly pointed the villagers to life.

Vulpine was just as pleased with the winning song. The bell beckoned to the villagers, and the crowd gathered for the unveiling of the winners. The Assemblymen huddled on the porch on that windy, gray day when the new banner was unfurled and the new village song was sung. The villagers were sure their leaders had chosen well as the song stirred their spirits just to hear it, and they were happy to sing its pledge to serve the village.

That evening at the inn, Vulpine snickered with Phineas over drinks about how easily the villagers had their minds taken off the King. "Our fathers got that old man to stay up on King's Hill and locked up his law book. Now, the Assembly has voted out his song and banner and replaced them with ones of our own choosing. Sometimes it's too easy, Phineas. The villagers elected me a member of the Assembly. The other members elected me lord of the Assembly," Vulpine crowed. "There is only one title left for me to attain." Vulpine reveled in the thought. "I'm practically already the king myself."

Chapter 3

Gabe's mind was still on the King, and he again reasoned with his family why the King had to still be living. Gabe looked at his father with pleading eyes. His father took a deep breath and conceded. "I propose you go on a hike, Gabe. Climb King's Hill. See if the King is there. Is that what you want?"

The boy's eyes brightened and his back straightened. "Yes, sir."

"Good then. If the King is dead, he won't be there. Then we'll know that the law was a nice idea thought up by the King who gave us our village, and he just died before he could do what he wrote there. If the King is there...well, that's unlikely, as he's dead, but I understand your need to put the question to rest for yourself."

"No one goes up King's Hill. Ever. It's always been off limits." Mother's flustered words revealed her concern over the planned adventure. "It was set apart for the King's use. I

18

heard Phineas Tract declare that the hill would be kept forever as a monument for the King, and it was to be undisturbed. You know they keep it guarded."

"If the guard won't let him past, well, at least he tried," Father offered as consolation.

"I'll go in the morning." It was decided.

Gabe was awake before dawn, trying to decide what qualified as morning so that he could get up and begin his expedition. He napped fitfully, listening for the sounds that would announce the day, but it was a smell that roused him. Mother's sleep had flitted away as well, and she arose extra early to prepare a raisin loaf for her son. She didn't like the idea of her son going off into the unknown. She always felt best when her family was all under the protective roof of their inn. She wrestled with her thoughts as she wrestled with the dough. "Worrying won't help a thing," she kept telling herself, the repetition soothing her.

Gabe followed the scent trail to the kitchen and eagerly gathered up the warm bread and hard cheese his mother set before him. "I'll eat on the path. I need to get going." His mother made no response, a statue gracing their kitchen. "I won't be long. I can be to the top in an hour if I go quickly," he added, trying to assuage her concerns. She nodded, slightly. He nodded back.

Gabe struck out east on the dirt road that ran from the village square to King's Hill. Even though the hill was just a few stone throws away from the inn, he felt like a pioneer—adventurous and alone. He had been alone before, but it felt different this time; it felt brave and unsure. Overriding his paradoxical emotions was just one thought, *If I see the King, what will I say to him?*

He reached the foot of the hill without having prepared an opening line. A toad landed on his left foot, distracting him from his thoughts. The toad hopped off just beyond him, and the natural impulse of a ten-year-old boy to try and catch it overpowered him. He lunged for it. Missed. Again. *Drat.* He crouched down low like a lioness ready to pounce. He waited until the toad was least suspecting. *Gotcha!*

"King's Hill is off limits. What are you doing here?" The guard demanded answers from the boy sprawled on the ground. Gabe held up the toad.

"Just trying to catch my toad." The reply slipped off his tongue. *Well, it is my toad now. I caught him,* he assured himself of the truth of the statement. The toad, without a sound, made a desperate attempt for escape and leapt to freedom. As if by reflex, Gabe again launched himself toward the toad. The guard snorted and retreated to his post. Gabe kept up the maneuvers until the guard was safely settled back in his guard box, comfortably seated on his stool.

Gabe thanked the toad for his help and made his way into the cover of the pines.

The encounter with the toad had relaxed him, and instead of trying to figure out what to say to the King, he explored his surroundings. Hidden among the dense needles of the pines, Gabe felt safe. He crouched and examined mushrooms, pine cones, rocks and beetles. Finding himself at the foot of an evergreen with low sweeping branches, he ducked underneath. Next to the trunk, he was able to stand up and move around. Imagining himself barricaded inside a fort, he opened his pack and dug into his rations.

Tasting the sweet raisins his mother had folded into his bread—a special treat for a special occasion—reminded him of his word to her that he wouldn't be long. He refocused on his task. *Climb the hill. Find the King's home. And...*He didn't know what came next. *Okay. One step at a time.* On his feet again, he raised his eyes and started to climb purposefully.

It was cold in the cover of the forest; the sun still low in the sky as Gabe walked through the trees. His eyes leapt to each movement in the forest. The animals, not accustomed to humans, bolted before Gabe, who couldn't catch a glimpse of any of them. He saw branches bend and heard leaves rustle, but the animals remained hidden.

The sun climbed higher, matching Gabe's achievement. Gabe soon came out of the pine forest and for the first time, laid eyes on the summit. He wasn't sure what he had thought. He realized he had no idea what to expect. He had heard the King lived in a golden palace.

A deer appeared from among the pines, and Gabe froze, hoping not to scare it away so he could watch it. The forest animals never dared to visit the village, and he was fascinated by this unusual sight. With minute movements, he slowly slipped down onto one knee in the dewy grass. The buck moved regally toward him. Closer. Closer. Gabe was astonished, electrified by this steadily approaching creature. Closer. Closer. He wasn't sure if he should be scared, except that he didn't feel fear. He felt awe. The buck stopped next to him, his powerful antlers declaring his dominance on the hill. Gabe gradually stretched his legs and straightened until he reached his full height and found himself looking into the eyes of the buck.

The magnificent creature turned and advanced across the hill. He paused. His towering trophy turned, and the buck looked again into the boy's eyes. He gave his antlers a shake and was off again, crossing and climbing the hillside. Gabe began to follow. *Is this buck escorting me?* The procession led in and out of bushes and other trees, but this time the animals didn't run. Rabbits, foxes, squirrels, mice, beavers, badgers…the animals came out from hiding and lined the parade route. A hawk settled on a tree. A cardinal in another. A nightingale. The boy gaped as a great brown bear lumbered out.

Gabe, the pioneer, the adventurer, the explorer, was certainly in uncharted waters now. He wasn't afraid though. It was exhilarating. Some of the animals began to fall in line and trail behind Gabe. With each step, Gabe grew taller, more confident; he felt like he was king of the forest, king of the hill.

All at once, the procession halted. Gabe tripped on the buck's left hind leg and fell. No matter. All of the animals had their heads on the ground—bowing. *What is happening?* Gabe peeled his face off the ground and looked up. The King stood before him.

Gabe scrambled to his feet and then froze. *The King. The King.* They were the only words spinning through his mind. *The King. The King.* Only seconds passed before the magnitude of the moment struck him. He sank to the ground and bowed, following the animals' example, and trembled.

"Welcome, Gabe. I've been waiting for you. I'm glad to see the toad and buck have done their jobs well." The King's voice was strong and calm, a kind voice but one that demanded respect. Gabe's body remained unmoving, but his mind raced. *He knows my name. The toad and buck did their jobs? The toad from this morning? What job?*

The King smiled and turned his back to Gabe. The animals raised themselves and frolicked and frisked their way back to their homes. "Join me." Gabe recognized the King's invitation as a command. He lifted his head and saw the King moving steadily toward a cave. Gabe jumped to his feet and walked in the King's footsteps.

Gabe gawked as they approached the King's home, amazed the King lived in a cave, but as he entered, his surprise grew further. The King took his place on the throne, and Gabe stood before him, twisting and turning to take in the glittering eyeful. The King sat quietly and let the boy have his fill of the room. Gabe's gaze found its way back to the King, and he hung his head in shame for staring so intently at everything. He could hear his mother scolding him for being so nosy.

"Why don't you look around? Feel free to touch anything you like and to ask questions if you find something interesting." The King seemed to know just what Gabe had been feeling and his shame lifted. He moved uneasily at first, afraid he'd be clumsy and break something, but soon his worries evaporated like the morning dew on the hill, and he explored the cave freely.

It didn't seem like a cave, though. Gabe touched the wall. *This isn't rock. It looks like gold.* "The walls of the cave are covered with gold," the King responded to his ponderings. Gabe nodded, astonished again at the King's ability to know just what he was thinking. Fixed in the wall were twelve jewels, forming a semi-circle around the throne, which stood in the center of the room. Gabe fingered one. *I might as well ask. He probably already knows I want to.* Gabe cleared his throat. The King patiently waited. Gabe cleared his throat again.

"What type of stone is this?" Gabe held his breath.

"Emerald. And that's sapphire. Ruby. Diamond." The King pointed to the different precious stones and named them all. "The throne is made from gold, so are the steps leading up to the throne."

Gabe just nodded. What could he say? He lived in a wooden house with wooden tables and chairs. He ate out of a wooden bowl with a wooden spoon. Here, his surroundings were surreal.

He made his way around the back of the throne and saw that there was one wooden object there, a cabinet. Examining it up close, Gabe realized the carvings in the wood were scenes from the village. He ran his finger through the crevices, tracing the square, the Hall, the school yard, the inn.

25

It was all there. Inside the cabinet was a single dish, a plate of pearl circumscribed with gold.

This time it was easier to ask. "Why is there only one plate here?" All at once, he felt foolish. *Only one person lives here. Why would there be more than one plate? Stupid.*

The King answered gently. "That plate has been reserved for a special guest."

"Oh."

"A guest from the village." The King was smiling broadly. "Why don't you take it out and have a closer look?" The King was enjoying himself.

Gabe delicately lifted the latch on the door, and it swung open. With extreme caution, he lifted the brittle looking plate off its stand. It was more elegant than fancy, holding no design apart from its trim. Gabe cautiously turned it over in his hands. Etched in gold on the back was his name, Gabriel. "My name." The whispered words escaped in his astonishment.

The King began to laugh now. "You're the special guest. I had the plate prepared for you."

He cradled the plate in his arms, just as he had Tabitha when she was first born. They felt the same -smooth and fragile. He gingerly made his way around the throne. He stood again before the King, and then, without being conscious of making a decision, decided to sit and stay

26

awhile. He folded his knees beneath him and sat at the King's feet. The plate rested in his lap. His eyes rested on the plate. Finally, he blurted out his question. "Why?"

"I'm always prepared to feed those who seek me." The King's answer was an enigma to Gabe, but he decided not to ask any further questions. In the wonder of the morning, Gabe had forgotten entirely his original purpose in coming. As he sat silently before the King, it all started to come back to him.

"They said you were dead." He plunged into his story, and the rest flowed as steady as a river into the sea. The King listened patiently. "And, I don't know, I just couldn't rest until I found you. They didn't think I would find you, but somehow I just knew you would be here. No one else believes you are alive, but I knew you just had to be." Gabe had been talking to the floor. He looked up and his heart melted. *He understands me. He loves me.*

Unthinking, he flung himself at the King's feet. The plate crashed to the floor and fractured into three pieces. Gabe wrapped his arms around the King's legs, and crying, he clung fast, sure he would never let go.

The King let him stay there, wet and clingy. Finally, Gabe, quieted and calmed, released his vice grip and sat up. He stared at the plate and felt ashamed again. The King stood and walked down the steps that led to his throne. He bent and

27

picked up the pieces, held them together for a moment and then handed the plate to Gabe, whole.

This time Gabe was speechless for a whole new reason; he was flabbergasted. Stunned, he stammered, "I…I…I'm sorry I broke the plate."

"Already fixed and forgotten." The King's light remark removed Gabe's shame. "Now, let me tell you more about this plate." The King spoke as he took his place again on his throne. Gabe settled in once more at the King's feet with the plate, this time, on the floor beside him. "This plate is my invitation to you to come and sup with me, anytime." Gabe smiled. "Sup with us" was just how his mother would say it, inviting in friends or strangers for a meal. "Come to me whenever you like, and I will see that you are never hungry."

Gabe felt full. "Could I come back tomorrow?" The King smiled and nodded.

Gabe placed his plate back onto its stand, his sign that he was always welcome to visit the King. He scuttled toward the door but stopped short of it. "Thank you," he said simply and ducked out the door without saying goodbye. He hadn't felt a need to. He'd be back tomorrow.

Chapter 4

Gabe stopped in front of the inn and tried to brush the dirt from his trousers. He removed his right shoe and shook a pebble from it. *How can I explain what just happened? What am I—* He didn't get to finish the thought. Angela had spotted him and ran out to greet him. Tabitha skipped along behind.

"What happened?" Angela asked.

"I found him."

"What?"

"I found the King. I...I..." His lips couldn't form the words. His tongue flapped uselessly, making odd monosyllabic noises. He didn't know how to begin.

"You found the King? How do you know? There was someone living on the hill? How do you know it wasn't someone else?"

"Impossible." Gabe found that question easy to answer. "There's no one like him. He knew my name. He knew what

29

I was thinking. He answered my questions before I asked them. He somehow fixed a plate I had broken by just holding it. He loved me." His voice dropped off, but the words didn't fall; they floated in the breeze and carried their warmth with them. Angela could almost feel the warmth of the King's love as the words washed over her face.

Butterflies began flitting around in Angela's stomach. "Mother's at the market. Father's paying a visit to Percy Katrid. Will you tell me all about the King?"

They sat on the ground, leaning their backs on the hard wood of the inn. He started at the beginning from when his first shoe hit the path until he had thanked the King. He told her every detail he could describe. He even confessed to clinging to the King and crying. Angela remained transfixed the whole time. When all was told, he sat quietly and imagined himself again at the King's feet. Finding the King alive should have raised more questions than it settled, but he was content. No more questions raged in him. He was at peace like the lake at sunrise on a cloudless winter day.

Tabitha twirled and watched her skirts fly out. Angela let Gabe sit in peace while she thoughtfully studied his face and determined something was different. She was sure something had happened to him up on the hill that morning.

"I believe you."

Gabe's thoughts were interrupted. "What?"

"I believe you."

It hadn't occurred to Gabe that his words could be unbelievable, but as he thought about it, he realized it all sounded crazy. He started to giggle at the absurd story of the dead King who's alive and reads minds and fixes plates and who actually only has one plate which happens to have his name on it. He realized the significance of his sister's affirmation.

"Thank you."

Angela smiled.

"Do you think anyone else will believe me?"

Angela shook her head. "It's a tall tale." She began laughing herself. "Do you think I could meet him?"

"I don't know. I'll ask him tomorrow. I'm going back. I'm going to go every day."

"Father's not going to let you skip your chores and learning to go climb that hill every day."

"I have to go. I don't know. The King has a way of helping me come to him. He'll help me get there."

Angela remembered the toad and the buck. "Right, I forgot. I'll help you too. I don't need to go. I can stay home and do your morning chores. You can meet with the King, and then you can tell me everything he—"

"Oh, Gabe, you're home." Their mother was barreling toward them, the bounty in her satchel threatening an avalanche. "Now don't you try that again. Only so much a mother's heart can take."

"Gabe met the King, and he did magic tricks." Tabitha's summary of his morning was not what he had expected to share with his mother. He began to object, but his mother spoke first.

"Telling your sister stories, I see. Anyhow, it's a good thing you are back here now. I just heard Lord Vulpine wants to hold another meeting tonight. We need to fix up a stew and get the room set." She blustered past them and set straight to work.

Gabe stood dumbfounded. *Make-believe stories. That's what she thinks. She doesn't know the truth. Does she want to know what really happened?* He realized his parents didn't consider for a moment that the King might still be alive. It wasn't a possibility to them. *How can I convince them he's alive?*

"Let's go help." Angela's words cut into his distressing thoughts but didn't cut loose their weight. He carried the burden as he trudged after his sister.

When Gabe's father returned home, events imitated those earlier with his mother. Neither had heard the truth, but neither asked for it.

That evening, while Vulpine commanded the audience of the Brothers and Sons, Gabe sought an audience with his father. He found him again hunched over his books. "Father, I want to go every day to King's Hill."

"What?" Gabe's father had been interrupted and his mind was elsewhere.

"I want to go up King's Hill every day. I want to see the King."

"The King? What do you mean?"

"I met the King today. He invited me back, and I want to go."

"Gabe, I don't know what you are talking about. The King is dead. If you enjoyed your hike, then fine, it would be good exercise for you to climb for a bit each day if the guard doesn't mind it. You'd have to go early in the morning and be back in time for chores and breakfast. But no talking with strangers."

"Yes, sir." His father had been quicker to respond than usual. He wasn't willing to ponder the possibility of the King living on the hill. Gabe withdrew from the room sullenly.

The next morning, Gabe was up and out before the sun had thrown off nighttime's cloak. He returned in time for breakfast but ate in silence. Afterward, as they plucked the apples from their family's trees and gathered them into bushels, he shared with Angela all the King had told him. Gabe was fast asleep before the candles in the inn had been blown out.

And so began a daily ritual of rising early, racing up the hill, sitting at the King's feet, and retracing his steps, usually in time for breakfast. Angela took up more and more of his chores and became a diligent disciple, taking in every word of the King as reported by Gabe.

The snows came, and Gabe rose in the dark when the shrill shrieking of scavenging rats could still be heard. Huddled in his cloak, he plowed his way down the road and up the hill. He never missed a chance to meet with the King. The King taught him the words of the book of law, explained the meanings behind the words and answered Gabe's questions.

"Are there others who come daily to visit you?"

"No. Sometimes there is someone who wanders up the hill a bit, seeking one thing or another, but only those who truly seek me are able to find me."

"Why don't they seek you?"

"They aren't willing to make the necessary sacrifices."

Gabe reflected over the past months: the early hours and lack of sleep, the long climb, the risk of being caught by the guard, the feeling of separation from all the other kids who had no interest in the King, his family not understanding his new life.

"Maybe it's a sacrifice," he conceded, "but it feels like a privilege."

"It's both, and it is also a responsibility."

Gabe didn't ask for an explanation. He was thinking of another question.

"What about Angela?" Gabe knew he didn't need to explain who she was. "She has sacrificed to get to know you, but she hasn't seen you."

"You're right. She has sacrificed her time and energy, and even though she hasn't seen me, do you think she has received some of the privileges of finding me?"

"Yes," Gabe answered simply; he knew it was true. He and Angela both had something that others lacked. They had peace and joy and both felt the King's love. They were gaining knowledge and wisdom about the world that even the leaders of the village wouldn't be able to match.

"Maybe if you would come down to the village, then people would know you are alive and would want to be with you. Why don't you come to the village?"

"The first day you came, I showed you your plate. It was your invitation to visit me as often as you like. The village withdrew their invitation to me. Not everyone is willing to make the sacrifices you have made to be with me, nor are they willing to accept the responsibility of knowing me and my law. But even so, I said I would come back one day, and I will."

Chapter 5

"Gabe, I want you to know something." Gabe was again at the King's feet and saw sadness in his eyes. He sat up straighter.

"A very severe hailstorm is going to strike the village. I'm telling you so you won't be frightened. People won't be suspecting it when the winds pick up. They'll think it is just an April shower. It will be coming soon. On a sunny day, when the winds suddenly pick up and a dark cloud covers the sun, I want you to go to your kitchen and stay there until the storm passes."

"When is it coming?" Gabe felt uneasy all of a sudden.

"Soon. Watch for the signs, and you'll be prepared."

"Yes, sir, but how will I convince my family? My parents don't even believe you exist."

"I'll make a way. Your family will be safe."

He had done it again, lifted the burden off Gabe. When Gabe returned home that day, he mentioned the storm to no

36

one but Angela. Over the next few days, the King didn't mention it again, so neither did Gabe.

Then one night, Gabe had a nightmare. He thrashed and sweated and cried out. Angela sat up with a start. She could almost feel Gabe's heart pounding as he sat up, panting. Tabitha was sleeping peacefully next to Angela when Mother rushed to his bedside.

"It's okay. It's okay." Mother tried to calm him. She stroked his hair to soothe her nerves as much as his.

"I had a dream. Mother, you can't go out today. There's going to be a hail storm. I saw it. A terrible storm. Hail big enough to knock a man down. The winds tore the banner off the Hall, and hail put holes in its roof. I saw roofs collapse and animals killed. You can't go out today."

"Gabe, what are you talking about? It was a dream. Relax. Let me go get you a warm cup of milk." She shuffled through the dark doorway and disappeared.

"Do you really think it will come today?" Angela asked.

Gabe tried to see Angela's form in the dark. "I think it might. He didn't tell me when, but he said he would help me make Mother and Father believe so they would be safe. Maybe that's why I had the dream. It was awful. I don't want to think about it anymore."

"Okay. It will be okay. The King will help us. Think about him. Think about King's Hill. You'll be able to go back to sleep."

He followed Angela's advice, relaxed and was asleep before Mother returned with the milk.

When the family gathered for breakfast, Mother told Father about their eventful night. He, like Tabitha, always did a good impersonation of a hibernating animal, sleeping no matter what was happening in the outside world. He listened to Mother and noticed the concern written in the wrinkles on Gabe's forehead.

"I'm glad it was just a dream. Don't worry about it." His father spoke nonchalantly. When his advice didn't soften the lines on Gabe's face, he added, "We can't just stop our lives because of a dream."

"It's not just the dream," Gabe said softly. "The King told me a terrible hailstorm was coming. He said when the winds picked up and the clouds blocked the sun, we were to go to our kitchen and wait out the storm." Gabe didn't dare look at anything above his toes.

"What?" His father was perplexed by what he was hearing.

Gabe didn't answer.

"What did you say?" Gabe's father never raised his voice, but there were times when Gabe felt like Father was yelling at him, and this was one of them.

"The King told me." The words fell to the floor.

"What are you saying?" The subject of the King had been dropped by the family months ago. His parents knew he went up the hill daily but that was all.

"The King told me." This time Gabe looked his father in the eyes and spoke each word deliberately.

His father was taken aback by his forthrightness and spoke softly in return. "When did you speak with the King?"

Gabe looked directly at his father. "I speak with the King every day. The King is alive and lives on the hill. You and Mother didn't believe me when I first went, so I've kept quiet about it."

"He's told me everything about the King," Angela added. "And I believe him. It's true."

"I have no idea what you are talking about." Mother's vexation was evident. She busied herself cleaning to avoid the conversation.

Father, however, was carried to a world away by Gabe's words. He watched his grandfather as he scrolled the words of the King's law. He flew to the summit of the hill, heavy laden with a King's golden throne. He heard the King's song and his banner flap in the breeze. He was remembering the

King. His world had faded away, and the reality of the King engulfed him. Taking in a gulp of air, Gabe's astonished father came to his senses and asked, "He lives?"

"He lives," Gabe answered authoritatively.

"He lives," Angela assured him, beaming.

Gabe and Angela watched the transformation come over their father with gleeful hearts. They knew the experience well. Gratefulness overwhelmed Gabe. Months of wishing for this moment, and here he was, a witness to it. Angela sighed a happy sigh and said, "This is the perfect day."

"When will you tell me about the King?" Gabe's father realized he was an infant in his knowledge.

"When we're huddled in the kitchen during the storm," Gabe decided. "The King has a way of—" Gabe started in but was promptly interrupted.

Mother's skirts brushed against the table as she swept past the others, fixing a scarf over her dark brown hair. "I'm going to market. I'm not staying home because of someone's imagination. Besides, what will everyone eat if I don't go?" She was out the door.

Father was worried. Angela set out to console him. "Gabe, didn't the King say your family would be safe during the storm?"

Gabe nodded toward Angela.

"Well," said Angela, "let's not worry. You taught me the King's word is always true."

"That's right." Father's memory was jolted. "You told us that right after you read the King's law. 'The King's words are sure and true.' I believe that's what you said. Don't know how I can remember that, but I'm glad I do. Let's believe the King's words and not worry."

"Yes, sir!" Gabe was feeling giddy, a rubber ball set loose from a great height. He felt like anything was possible. No fears were lurking inside. *The King will keep Mother safe.*

Mother had already left the inn, but Father, along with Gabe and Angela, agreed to stay home for the rest of the day. Keeping Tabitha with them would not present a problem.

There was no sign of a storm. The sun was a golden medallion adorning a cloudless blue sky. The family busied themselves with chores around the inn. Gabe chopped and stacked firewood which would be needed for the stove, even when the weather warmed. Angela swept the floors and peeled potatoes. They worked silently, but they knew what the other was thinking. *When's the storm going to come?*

Crash! Tabitha shrieked. Bang! "Tabitha, go sit at the kitchen table and don't leave." Tabitha was so surprised by Angela's commanding tone that she quickly obeyed the order. Gabe had dashed out the front door of the inn and skidded to a halt. Angela quickly fell in behind him. The

41

landscape was staggering, even though they had been warned. The sun was gone, swallowed whole by the threatening mass of a cumulonimbus, hovering, dwarfing the village like a giant boot about to squash a bug.

The inn's sign was knocking against the eave, its metal chains jangling. In a pine just in front of the inn, a red crossbill wrapped protective wings around her eggs and braced to defend her nest against the storm. Gabe's gaze turned to King's Hill. It seemed the storm skirted along its edges; the peak was reaching up to the clear blue heavens. *The King was somehow in control of this storm.* Gabe didn't understand the thought, but it was a comforting one anyway.

The dusty road had become more whirlpool than walkway, dirt fiercely swirling, not caring who was pummeled by its pebbles. Their next-door neighbor passed by. "Can you believe this wind?"

Gabe hollered back, "Get inside, Mr. Bollix, and stay there! This is going to be a bad storm!"

"I've seen worse. Funny how suddenly the wind picked up. I'm on my way home now. We'll be seeing you." He shielded his eyes from the onslaught of dust.

Gabe was startled by the man's composure. Gabe wanted to tear through the streets telling everyone to take cover. Thinking of Mother, he felt helpless. The vanished fears were slowly creeping back.

Father rushed to the door and herded his children away from the whipping winds. He had brought Betty inside. The incongruous sight made Gabe laugh out loud. "What would Mother say if she saw a cow in the dining hall?" The laughter left his lips with the words. *Mother.* The three of them stood in silence. Then it began.

Thud. Thud. Thud. A heavy fist was pounding the roof. They looked up at the ceiling and then at each other. *Hail.* "Let's get into the kitchen." Their father shepherded the children to the kitchen where Tabitha was waiting at the table. Inside, the only movement was the kitchen door swinging back and forth. Outside, the storm was a rampaging drunk, toppling everything within its reach, its fury crashing and splintering all it touched.

Thump. Rattle. The three tried to ignore the percussion symphony playing for them outside, especially the hail which was using the inn as a kettle drum. They distracted themselves with talk of the King.

Father looked to Gabe. "I don't know where to begin, what to ask. What do you want to tell me about the King?"

Apart from having his mother sitting across from him right then asking the same question, there was nothing more Gabe wanted. "Remember the old village song? The line, *His love's a banner waving over all of us.*"

"Of course, *His love's a banner waving over all of us, a beacon leading us out of our darkest night.*" Tabitha didn't recognize the words.

"Well, that song was about the King, right?" Gabe was enjoying his role as teacher. "It tells us about him. He is love. When you are with him, you feel loved. I don't know how to describe it, except I think we all feel it right now."

It was true. They all looked at each other and loved each other. It was more than the requisite love of family bonds. It was deeper and purer and more unalterable than any of them could describe.

"Why does the village have a new song now?" Angela asked. "The old one was so beautiful. Why did they change it?"

"I think I know," Father answered with a sigh. "I'm realizing it all right now. I was blind to it before. Obviously if the King is alive, we were lied to by our leaders. They were also the ones behind taking away the song that taught us about the King. It's just as before. I bet my father was right that the village leaders asked the King not to return. They didn't want to compete with him for authority over the village. They are doing the same now. They want to get rid of the King so they can rule."

"But Father, they already rule the village. The King hasn't been involved in years and years. I don't understand."

44

"Angela, there's a difference between elected officials making laws and rulers who usurp power and abuse authority." Father's gaze was fixed hard at the far wall. "I couldn't see it before."

"I don't understand what you're talking about."

"Lord Vulpine."

"What?" Angela couldn't follow her father's thinking.

"Lord Vulpine wants to be king."

"I'm lost, Father. What are you talking about?"

"I'm sorry, Angela. I'm just realizing it all and still trying to put the pieces together. Lord Vulpine convinced everyone the King is dead. They changed the village banner and song to erase any memory of the King. Vulpine has been working through the Assembly, but somehow I bet he's going to figure out a way around them so that he alone holds power over the village."

"What's he going to do?" Angela asked, worried.

"I have no idea. But it is obvious he wants the King dead. Then he could be sure there wouldn't be any opposition from the outside to his taking power."

"We don't have to worry about the King." Gabe interrupted the discussion. "There's no way they could kill him. He's untouchable. Even today, his throne sits above the clouds. If this storm can't touch him, Vulpine can't either."

Everyone's focus was brought back to the storm. "Where do you think Mother is?" Angela asked what was now on everyone's mind.

THE KING WILL MAKE A WAY

Chapter 6

It took almost half an hour for the drunken man to plunge into a stupor. The village lay deathly still. Taking Tabitha by the hand, Father led the way outside, removing his family from the protection of the inn. They were aghast. The village looked like a forest after loggers had come through. It had been ripped, torn, tossed, tumbled, shaken, crushed, knocked down, as if it had been a bowling pin and the hail had rolled a strike.

"I'm going to take a look around the inn. You three just stay here." Father began inspecting their property and disappeared around a corner.

"Where's Mother?" Tabitha whined.

"She'll be home in a minute." Angela tried to sound confident.

A woman screamed. Three heads snapped in the direction of their neighbors. "I'm going to help." Gabe sprinted past the edge of the inn and leapt over the wood pile which used to be the fence surrounding the Bollix property. The fence had been built to keep out danger, but it had failed to thwart the storm.

"Mrs. Bollix? Where are you? What's wrong?" He stopped to listen. Sobs. Gabe took off toward the barn. One glance through the open door told the story. He went numb. Mrs. Bollix rocked back and forth; her body convulsed with sobbing. Mr. Bollix lay motionless under heavy rafters, a portion of the barn roof now missing where it had once used its strength to shelter. Light poured in from the collapsed roof; the sun went on shining, acting as if nothing had happened.

"Mrs. Bollix, I..." Gabe's words caught in his throat. What could he say? "I'm sorry" was all he could manage. *Some help I'm being.*

Mrs. Bollix slowed her rocking and for the first time acknowledged her company. "There's nothing you could have done to help. He was dead by the time I found him." A torrent of tears started up again.

Gabe was at a loss. *What can I do? What could I have done? I warned him it would be a bad storm and told him to stay inside.* Guilt crept up from the base of his spine until the weight of it caused his head to hang in shame. He could have told him about the King and his words.

"Mrs. Bollix?" She didn't respond. Gabe went to her and knelt at her side. "Mrs. Bollix?" She slowly calmed herself again and turned and looked at him with vacant eyes.

"Mrs. Bollix, I'm sorry because I knew the storm was coming, and I knew it would be bad, and I didn't tell your husband and warn him ahead of time. It's my fault."

"What are you talking about? No one knew a hailstorm was coming. You saw how fast it came on. You couldn't have done anything."

"I did know. The King told me. The King, the King of our village is alive, and he knew, and he told me."

"I don't know what you're talking about. Leave me in peace here. My head is throbbing, and you're talking like a madman."

Unsure of what to say or do, he started toward the door. "I'll ask my father to come help." He spoke to the hay and ducked outside. He ran back to the inn. No one was waiting out front anymore. He went inside trying to find someone. Betty was no longer in the dining hall. He heard a voice in the kitchen. *Mother?*

He pushed forcefully on the door causing it to slap back hard in the opposite direction. His mother was at the table pouring out her story.

"The wind was blowing strong, and I had my bag full of vegetables. I thought of Gabe and decided to come right

49

home. But I wasn't fast enough, and hail started to rain down while I was still in the square. Did you see the hail? They were huge balls. I was running and running to get to the Hall. I saw the wind rip the banner right off the roof before I ducked inside. I waited there for the storm to end, but after a bit, a hail stone the size of a melon came crashing through the roof! I'm not exaggerating. It's the truth. It broke through the roof, but not only that, it landed right on the glass case that holds the King's law book. It shattered the case, completely destroyed it. Lord Vulpine was there, and he picked up the law book right away, which I thought showed a lot of care, and he told me to have the inn ready for another meeting tonight."

Gabe shot his father a distressed look. Father spoke up. "They can't have their meetings here anymore. Something has come up. I'll explain later. I'll go tell him myself. You stay here and recover."

Gabe and Angela excused themselves with Father, leaving Tabitha behind to keep Mother company.

"Father, I know you are on an errand, but I told Mrs. Bollix that you would help her. Mr. Bollix was killed by the storm. Part of his barn roof fell on him." Angela gasped in disbelief.

Father looked at the ground, shaking his head. "I wonder what else has happened. I'll send his brother over. I don't know what else has happened out there. Maybe you two should stay home."

Angela was distraught over her friend's loss and requested, "Please let me go check on Sally and stay with her and Mrs. Bollix until her uncle comes."

Gabe asked too. "Please let me go and see who needs help. What if we are the only ones who were safe?"

"Not only safe, but the inn didn't really suffer much damage. I don't know how, but the King really took care of us. Okay you two, go see if you can help."

Father set off to speak with Vulpine and Mrs. Bollix's brother-in-law. Angela retraced Gabe's steps to their neighbors. Gabe remained a moment surveying the scene; the backdrop was the same, but the props were all different. The road was littered with branches and fence posts. Trees were now stumps, fences kindling, roofs floors. The hail had been cannonballs fired upon an unsuspecting enemy. Several shots had struck down animals left out to pasture.

Gabe headed across the road, picking up debris as he went and calling out to see if anyone needed help. He worked cleaning up yards the rest of the day. In the evening, Father sat with a block of wood whittling while Gabe told him about the King. Father now joined Angela as a disciple, learning everything the King had told Gabe.

Gabe asked his father, "Do you want to come up and meet the King?"

Father took a deep breath and looked up at the ceiling. He shook his head slowly, one time left then right. "No, Gabe. I couldn't. I don't know. Honestly, I feel almost scared to meet him. It doesn't seem my place. We can learn from you. The King gave you an invitation to come whenever you wanted. You should be the one going."

Gabe nodded. He loved having an invitation to visit the King, but now he began to realize the responsibility that came with it.

Mother came into the dining hall where they were sitting together. "What are you doing, lollygagging around? Doesn't anyone have work to do?"

Father answered her. "We are working. We are learning. Why don't you sit and listen to Gabe tell us about his visits with the King?"

"Nonsense. Someone has to work around here. There's always work to be done." Mother was off in a huff.

The three looked at each other but didn't speak until Gabe continued teaching about the King. The scene was repeated the next day.

"Why are you pretending to work at that whittling? You use that as an excuse to sit around. We have enough of your creations gathering dust. Do we really need more?"

Father patiently responded, "You never know. Maybe someday we'll sell them, and they will be valuable to us. Why don't you take a break and sit with us? Gabe has some fascinating lessons to teach us."

"I don't need my son teaching me lessons. Where's the dignity in having your son for a teacher?" Father didn't take offense at Mother's words because he knew it wasn't really him that she was upset with, just the talk of the King. Mother's frustration grew as the days passed.

The spring rain showered. The summer heat scorched. The fall apples ripened. The lake froze. The flowers bloomed. The corn was knee high. The harvest was gathered. Snow drifted; eggs hatched; bees buzzed; leaves tumbled. The seasons and years flew by as Gabe faithfully visited the King. Angela was well versed in the King's law and was becoming a lady.

For three years Gabe sat still at the King's feet, but Vulpine was on the move. He prowled around the village, watching, observing, making sure he had his finger on the pulse of the villagers in order to steer them in the direction of his choosing. He was certain the key to controlling the villagers was to direct their gossip, the talk of the village, what was on everyone's mind.

To achieve this end, he often fed words to Phineas which he then regurgitated in the square. "Lord Vulpine won a great victory for our village in the Assembly yesterday." "Lord Vulpine makes sure the prices are fair at the market." "Lord Vulpine is always working for what's best for our village." The members of the Brothers and Sons secret society would repeat Phineas' words or, more accurately, Vulpine's, as they milled about the well, while they shopped in the market and when they welcomed guests into their homes. Most villagers were unwittingly dutiful in repeating the platitudes until they were branded onto their minds, and at that point, they became truth no matter their accuracy.

One day, Phineas carefully left out Vulpine's name from the announcement. Vulpine had easily convinced the other elected village leaders that elections weren't in the best interest of the village. Assemblyman Stone, never without his pipe, was the first to shake Vulpine's hand to congratulate him on the new law. Phineas explained the ruling to the villagers from the porch that ran the front length of the Hall. "Today, the Assembly has voted to end the village's annual elections. In order to maintain continuity within the village, your current elected leaders will serve until death." He assured the crowd gathered in the square that this was for peace and unity within the village. Everyone agreed that peace and unity were desirable and welcomed the new law.

Percy Katrid, a friend of Gabe's father, took notice of Vulpine's maneuvers. A handsome man, tall and broad, he won the admiration of many just by standing there. He may have been past his prime in strength and agility, but his physique maintained its powerful presence. His mind hadn't lost its edge either. It didn't escape Percy how Vulpine always managed to find a way for his name to be mentioned, or how Vulpine always took credit for any positive change in the village. Vulpine seemed to be praised even for the weather, when it was good. When the weather turned sour, or just plain strange as it often had over those few years, Phineas would keep force feeding lines to the villagers. "Lord Vulpine wants to see the drought end quickly!" The crowd would cheer their agreement. Percy Katrid thought the comment and the crowd's reaction inane. "Imbeciles, everyone wants the drought to end," he would mutter to no one. By seeding comments here and there, he found others similarly disaffected. But none of them, not even Percy, had an inkling of what Vulpine was planning for the coming winter.

Chapter 7

The harvest had been gathered and stored, and the time Vulpine had been patiently waiting for was fast approaching. He knew the rewards of delaying gratification and took pains not to move too soon.

The Brothers and Sons had gathered and heard Vulpine's instructions. They were each to store up in their homes one month's worth of food and supplies by midwinter. The rain had been sparse that summer, so the harvest was as well, and they were to all buy their bulk now while the farmers still felt amply supplied. They were told to anticipate the markets being closed during the winter, so they wouldn't be able to rely, as they normally would, on the farmers selling food in the stalls. Although there were men of many trades among the Brothers and Sons, including other Assemblymen, not one was a farmer, and so none had their own stores of food.

They weren't told why the market would close. In the whispered sessions, only the broad aspects of Vulpine's plans

56

were shared. The details were told only to those who needed to know. This time it would again be the village doctor who would be assisting Vulpine. As a member of the Brothers and Sons, he was obliged to use all that was in his power to serve Vulpine and help him become king. Years of work had gone into the planning and maneuvering. The doctor's help would now bring him one step closer to what he had long desired.

Vulpine had asked the doctor if he could prepare a plague. Vulpine explained the practicality of the request. The villagers needed to feel weak and scared so they would embrace a leader—a king. The summer drought had helped but hadn't been enough. He wanted a sickness that would spread easily and be serious enough to kill, not the entire village, just enough to create the fear he needed to harness for his own ends. The village doctor, though employed to save lives, fulfilled the request.

He figured he could meet Vulpine's requirements by dipping an arrow into the decomposing bodies of villagers who had died of their illnesses and then causing someone to be "accidentally" shot with the poisoned arrow. It was planned that the virus would be unleashed midwinter.

Phineas crunched through the autumn leaves on his way to the square and from the Hall announced that over the winter months, when the farm work was slow, the men of the village were to take part in military training. The village had

57

never before had any sort of army, nor had they ever been attacked by enemies, but Vulpine had convinced the Assembly of the need for a trained force.

Gabe would turn fourteen over the winter and was too young to be considered man enough to join in the training. His father, however, took part in the daily drills. He marched, practiced sword play, shot arrows and learned to fire a cannon. Percy Katrid also trained with the others and played the part of a submitted soldier. While he felt devotion to the village in which he was born and raised, he felt none towards Vulpine, who presided over the training exercises.

As lord of the Assembly, Vulpine took it upon himself to name a general for the village defenses. He named a Jeremy Writ, one of the members of the Brothers and Sons. He was a lanky man, an intellectual who saw the profit in serving Vulpine. General Writ was appointed not for his expertise but for quite another reason. He would do Vulpine's bidding without question.

Vulpine was pleased with how this new phase of his plan was progressing and gave the doctor the nod in midwinter. Just as had been planned, one of the Brothers and Sons accidently shot one of his fellow soldiers in the leg with an infected arrow. Soon a virus began to spread. Men were falling ill, experiencing delirium from unusually high fevers and weakness from vomiting. The illness lasted five whole days at a time. The drills were halted after one of the sick soldiers died, and the men were sent home to rest, which resulted in bringing the virus to their families.

As a result, the village effectually shut down as the villagers fell prey to the sickness. The virus made its way through the village like locusts, devouring all the life in its path. Panic started to set in as several children died from the sudden illness. Vulpine suspended the regular meetings of the Assembly and went into hiding.

Gabe's father had returned home sick, and Tabitha and Angela had taken ill along with him. Gabe nursed them back to health. Mother stayed away but prepared broths for them to sip while they still lay in bed. Gabe constantly toted water from the well behind the inn, through the kitchen, up the stairs and into the family quarters in order to sponge the victims with cool water to bring down their temperatures and to wash their clothes and bedding after their stomachs wretched violently. Gabe had never seen Angela so quietly submissive as during those days when he would ask her to sit or roll over or whatever was necessary for his nursing care.

Gabe still sneaked away each day in the quiet of the morning when everyone was finally settled and sleeping peacefully. The King had reassured him that his father and sisters would all live through the sickness and that he and his mother would not succumb to it. He believed the King, and he never hesitated to be at their sick beds, ready to help in any way he could. In a week's time they had come through safely, and in another week's time they were out of bed, fully recovered.

As Father and the girls were gaining back their full strength, the King had some questions for Gabe. "What would you want someone to do for you if you were sick, or if your parents were sick?" The King had a plan and was gently leading Gabe on the right path.

Gabe thought it over. "I would want someone to take care of me, to help me, to do my chores, to cook my meals and to tell me that I was going to be okay."

In a teacherly fashion, the King asked, "What does my law say about the things we would want others to do for us?"

Gabe knew the answer. "It says that we should do to others what we would want them to do to us."

"So what are you going to do?" The King nudged Gabe toward applying his knowledge.

"I'm going to help others."

"How?" the King asked encouragingly.

"I'll help people take care of their work in their homes and do my best to comfort them."

"Good." The King approved Gabe's plan, which had been the King's plan all along, and Gabe grew eager to get started.

He had one big hurdle to overcome before he could follow through on his word to the King; he had to convince his parents to let him go into the homes of the sick. Most people avoided all contact with others and shut themselves into their homes. The square now echoed in emptiness instead of vibrating with life. The villagers lived in fear and looked out only for themselves. Some villagers even refused to care for their sick family members and quarantined them in rooms in their own homes, leaving them to suffer alone.

Only two weeks had passed since Father had fallen ill and had been sent home to recuperate. The virus had spread like a juicy bit of gossip and had paid a visit to most homes in the village. Shops were closed and the market was bare, both for fear of the contagion and for lack of sellers and shoppers since the majority of the village was sick or had been sick with the violent virus. Only the families of the members of the Brothers and Sons had been conveniently shut safely in their homes at the beginning of the outbreak.

No one else in the village was tending to the sick outside of their own families, but Gabe persuaded his parents that he was immune to the sickness as he had been exposed to it during their family's bout with the plague and hadn't caught it. Angela took up the cause and suggested that Gabe might be able to bring home some food other than the family's stored apples and staples they had been forced to begin living on. Their parents saw both their points and relented to let Gabe go alone. They were unsure of how desperate people were and how they would act, and they wanted to keep Angela safe at home.

Gabe and Angela were bursting with excitement to begin helping. They had decided they would start with their nearest neighbors and work house to house down the road for as long as they were needed. Angela would be in charge of preparing food for Gabe to take to neighbors. It wouldn't be an easy task as Mother wouldn't allow Angela to use anything from their stock other than flour and salt for the job. Mother wanted to be sure the family had all they needed to last through the plague, for which there was no end in sight. It was like an unwelcome houseguest taking up residence without any mention of when he will be moving on.

Angela tied Mother's apron around her waist and, taking a wooden cup from the cupboard, she dug it into the flour barrel. Four times she dumped its contents into a large bowl. With her hands she squeezed in a hunk of butter she had made herself. She was thankful for the constant supply of milk, butter and cheese Betty provided the family. She rolled the butter and flour between her fingers until each had disappeared into the other. A little at a time, she added water and stirred it sparingly until the dough would hold together. Dusting the table with flour, she used the surface to roll the dough out as thin as she dared. She sprinkled on salt and slid it into the oven. It would make a crispy cracker, a perfect complement to the soup she was preparing.

Next Angela turned to the pot on the stove. She salted the water and begged a bit of seasoning from Mother. On the stovetop next to the simmering water, Angela heated a pan and poured in a cup of oil, dredged from Mother's cooking pots. When the oil had been heated, its fragrance wafted through the air, telling Angela it was time to add in a cup of flour. Stirring vigorously, Angela watched the flour bubble in the oil and turn a rich brown, the aroma of roasted wheat filling the kitchen. With one movement she lifted the pan and poured it into bubbling broth. It hissed and spat as the oil and water quarreled. Angela briskly stirred them together and ended the dispute. The flour thickened the broth so that it would cling to the crisping crackers.

Gabe filled two jars with the soup, wrapped a napkin around some crackers and headed out the door. He stood in the chill of the afternoon and let the sun warm his cheeks. How could such a beautiful day hold death in its air?

Chapter 8

Gabe knocked on the door of the Bollix family farmhouse. Angela's friend Sally answered the door.

"Gabe, welcome. Is everything okay? How is your family?"

Gabe smiled, thinking he had come to ask the same questions. "We're okay. Do you need any food?" Gabe held out his offering of warm soup and crackers.

Sally reached out and took the jars and napkin. "Thank you, Gabe. My mother is sick, and I'm taking care of my brothers and sisters myself. We have our harvest stored up here if you need some food, but this meal will help me. I appreciate it."

"If you could spare some food for us, we could really use it."

"Of course." Sally helped him home with bags of potatoes and carrots.

"Thank you so much," Gabe said, expressing his gratitude. "We'll be sure to use some of this to make food for other families as well."

"I'm glad to help. Thanks for coming, Gabe. I'm glad you came to check on us." Sally headed back into her home and closed the door.

Gabe's parents were pleased with Gabe's first attempt at helping and didn't stop him from going out again. Gabe approached the next house and knocked on the door while balancing soup and crackers in one hand.

A small boy opened the door. Gabe asked where his mother and father were. He just stared at Gabe, not answering. He still made no sound when Gabe entered the house to look around. "Hello?" Gabe called repeatedly, shivering in the chill of the house. The little boy tagged along as Gabe went in search of someone, anyone in the house.

Gabe found a room with a woman lying in bed with a baby. He stood frozen, not knowing if he should enter. Gabe continued calling out, but he received no answer. He looked again at the little boy and asked, "Is this your mother?" The boy nodded. "Where is your father?" The boy only shook his head no.

Gabe swallowed hard, hoping that didn't mean the boy's father was dead. *Is his mother alive?* He looked once more at the still bodies in the room and swallowed hard again.

Grimacing, he moved haltingly across the room to the bed. He called out his timid greeting again. There was no response. He tried one last time, and the mother stirred and mumbled.

Gabe backed away to the room entrance. "I brought some food." Gabe felt foolish saying the words, but he had no idea what to do. He looked at the little boy and added, "I'll keep your little boy with me until you are better." The woman gave Gabe no recognition. Gabe was at a loss and stood there in silence.

Gabe shivered again and came to his senses. He quickly started a fire in the fireplace and taking the boy by the hand, left the house. The boy made no objection to following Gabe home, and Mother recognized him immediately when Gabe entered the inn.

Everyone agreed something had to be done. Mother wanted to help the woman, but she didn't want to risk getting sick. Angela and Father, immune from having been sick, went together to take back the broth and see how they could help. It didn't take them long to discover that the woman was very ill and the baby was dead. Father had the morose chore of burying her baby.

The little boy remained with Mother as Gabe went to the next farmhouse. This time he was met by shouts to go away.

Gabe's enthusiasm for helping was waning, and he carried on only out of his love for the King and his desire to please him.

At the next farmhouse, he was greeted by the matriarch of the family. "My name is Emily. I would be grateful if you would help us."

She told Gabe how their youngest son had died from the virus, and John, their only other son, was now in bed with the fiendish fever. She was concerned her husband was trying to work too hard when he himself was recovering from illness.

"We are reliant on John for so much," his mother confessed. "We would be so thankful if you could spare a bit of time to help some." Gabe lent his services in chopping wood and milking cows before heading to the next farm.

At the next home, he carried water and moved a mattress. Some of the farmers gave Gabe food for his own family, but at other homes he wasn't welcome at all.

To go to the shopkeepers' homes, he borrowed a cart from the Bollix family to carry Angela's soup pot. He pulled the cart slowly over the road to the square. At first glance, he thought that all the shops in the Square were closed, but as he walked along one row, he saw the village doctor through a window. He was sitting with his head in his hands.

Gabe pushed open the door, and the doctor quickly looked up like a child caught with his hand in the cookie jar. He cleared his throat and asked Gabe how he could help him.

"Actually, I came to help," Gabe answered. "Do you need food?" Gabe pointed to the pot.

"Yes, thank you. It's impossible to buy any food these days." The doctor found a bowl, and Gabe ladled in the potato soup which Angela had prepared from Sally's gift. Gabe handed him a cracker and apologized there wasn't more.

"No, it's wonderful," the doctor insisted. "It's been a tough few weeks for me. I'm afraid you caught me hiding out. Everyone thinks the square is empty. I just wanted a moment's rest."

Gabe smiled and nodded. "I should go see if I can find anyone else needing food."

"That's very good of you," the doctor said in farewell.

Gabe didn't reply and pulled open the door. He looked back at the doctor, who had resumed the position Gabe had found him in, slumped over with his head in his hands. Gabe looked at him sadly and then pushed on across the square.

Door to door like a desperate salesman, Gabe offered his soup until the pot was scooped clean and dry. Even without the soup, he continued to offer help and to ask what people needed. He told some he would try to return the next day with more food.

He eventually came to a row of tall, fine houses. He knocked on the door of one of the beautiful homes. A servant opened the door and curtly asked Gabe his business. He offered help meekly, as he'd done at so many other homes, but his proffer was met with a gruff reply.

"The good doctor has servants to help him and a stock room full of food and supplies. He doesn't need help from someone like you." He shut the door in Gabe's face. Gabe stepped back and shook his head in confusion. He backed away and decided it was time to return home.

That night Gabe shared his mattress on the floor with the neighbor boy. His mother had been brought over to the inn as well and was settled into one of the empty guest rooms where she was recovering from her illness and the shock of losing her husband and baby.

When morning came, Angela prepared more soup and crackers, and Gabe returned as promised to the homes on the far side of the square. The inn quickly became known as a place of refuge and help. Over the next few weeks as the virus took its final toll on the village, people would sometimes make their way to the inn, looking for food, shelter or a helping hand. Everyone who came found all three.

As winter's sharp edge softened and spring breezes started to blow across the village, hopes began to rise that the wind was sweeping the virus away. Slowly, life began returning to the village. Windows, shuttered for weeks, opened to air out the stale homes. Villagers breathed easy again and fear was disappearing along with the winter frosts.

Gabe sloshed through the mud at the base of the mountain on his way again to meet with the King. He would finally ask his burning question.

"Why?" Gabe was sitting at the King's feet, talking with him about the plague of sickness that had paralyzed the village. "Why did the whole village suffer? Why did my family get sick, and I didn't?"

The King looked sympathetically at Gabe. He knew he couldn't comprehend the full answer, but he wanted to help him understand what he could.

"Did the virus harm your family?" The King put the question to Gabe.

Gabe didn't answer right away. His sisters throwing up seemed like being harmed, but now he knew they were no worse off than before. He also knew that Angela was allowed to help others because of her immunity and that since her illness, a sort of quietness had come over her. She didn't always have an answer ready; it made her seem more gentle. "I guess not," he ventured to answer.

"Did the virus harm the village?" The King looked kindly at his pupil.

Gabe was sure the answer was yes. "It did harm the village. They say close to two hundred people died. Many were children. That's harm."

"Did the village deserve the harm that came to it?" The King's eyes were serious.

Gabe didn't know how to answer that one. He thought of his neighbor's lifeless baby and replied, "How could a little baby deserve to be killed? It didn't even know right from wrong. How could it deserve to be harmed?"

"Not the baby, Gabe. The village. Did the village deserve the harm that came to it?"

Gabe shook his head. "I don't know. I know the village doesn't follow your laws. Does that mean the villagers deserve to be harmed?"

"What does my law say is the penalty for not obeying it?" The King forced Gabe to look directly into his eyes.

Gabe thought through all he had been taught and knew the consequences of disobedience were great. "Just about everything that could go wrong is a penalty: not having enough food, sickness, being killed, drought and fierce weather in the village."

The King nodded. "I know you don't fully understand why the village has to suffer the penalty and not just the individual, but the individual matters too. I knew and told you that you would not catch the illness, and maybe those

71

children who died were being spared something worse. Remember that I'm always just. I am the only one who really knows what judgments and punishments are right and necessary. And never forget my song. I love the village. The villagers need to know that things are not all right the way they are."

Gabe nodded and felt like he understood a little better, except for one more thing.

"How do you do it? How do you judge what people are doing from here? How do you punish those not obeying your law from your throne room? How do you control something like a sickness?" Gabe's question multiplied into many on his tongue.

The King gently replied, "That's not something I can explain, but you can find comfort in knowing that however I do it, I can."

Gabe nodded and knew the King was right. Some things about the King were just too mysterious for someone like him to understand.

Chapter 9

The village returned somewhat to normal. The loss of lives left many gaps unfilled in homes and hearts. Vulpine was pleased with the results of his experiment with the doctor and prepared to make his final move to become king.

Gabe, unaware he would never again climb the hill to meet the King, sat in front of the throne like every other day before the sun had the chance to warm the village.

The King had a question for Gabe. "When you were younger and your father disciplined you for disobedience, what did you do after you received your discipline?"

Gabe was used to the King leading him to a lesson in this way and was anxious to find out what the King was getting at. "I obeyed whatever I hadn't before."

"Of course, that's the purpose of discipline. Do you remember our talk about the village disobeying my laws and receiving what was just in return?" Gabe nodded. "They disobeyed my laws. Do you think any learned their lesson from the discipline of the plague?"

A hint of a smile showed on Gabe's face. He understood. "You do love the village. You weren't just punishing them. You were disciplining them to teach them to obey your laws."

"Yes. Some will learn their lesson. Some will foolishly reject it. But now, who will teach them my laws so they can obey them?"

Gabe's smile faded, and he bit his lip. "I guess that would be me." They sat in silence a minute. The King knew Gabe's mind was wrestling. "But I don't know what to say. I tried telling Mrs. Bollix about you, and she told me to leave her alone. My mother won't listen to me. How can I convince anyone you are even alive so that I can get them to listen about your law?"

"Have I ever made the way for you before?"

Gabe laughed. "Lots of times. Okay. I'll try."

"Don't be afraid. I will make a way." The King's gentle eyes caught Gabe's and held them. "I always make a way."

Gabe smiled weakly and nodded. "I better get started before I lose my courage." That is what he said, but he wasn't feeling particularly courageous.

As Gabe stood to leave the throne room, the King gave him a reminder. "Don't forget that you aren't alone in this. You'll see me again."

"I know I'm not alone. I won't forget."

Gabe ran down the mountain, but his heart was pounding because of the task the King had given him. He decided that trying again at Mrs. Bollix's house was the best way to conquer his fear. The sun hadn't long been up when he knocked on the door and was invited in by Sally.

He stood waiting for Mrs. Bollix to join them and to give him permission to speak. "Mrs. Bollix, I apologized to you years ago when your husband died. I told you I was sorry because the King had told me the storm was coming, and I didn't warn you. What I said is true. The former King is alive, and I meet with him every day up on King's Hill, and he told me the storm was coming and that it would be bad. He told me to get in our kitchen and stay there when the winds picked up. I didn't tell anyone but my family. They were all safe and our inn was undamaged. The King kept us safe."

Mrs. Bollix sat quietly and fixed her gaze on the boy. She'd known him his whole life, and here he stood before her, a young man, full of a confidence she'd never seen in him before this moment. "I almost believe you," she said softly, but then her voice emptied of life. "But none of it matters now, does it? I don't hold his death against you."

At first Gabe agreed with her. *It didn't matter now. It was too late.* But then a light dawned on Gabe's face. "It does matter. You matter. You can choose to believe. I can teach you the King's law. It's not too late for you to listen to the King."

His earnestness took her aback. There were times she'd thought he couldn't put together more than two words. Now here he was, addressing her passionately. There was something else. She felt his compassion toward her, as if he truly cared.

"Okay," she said. "You can teach me about the King's law. I will listen to you. Come whenever you please."

"Thank you, Mrs. Bollix. Why don't you and your children join us at the inn this evening. Every night I teach my father and Angela about the King. Come. We can share a meal, and I will teach about the King's law."

"We will. Thank you."

The old Gabe was back. He gave a nod and wordlessly made his exit. He exhaled when he got outside, then made a beeline for another farmhouse. He remembered the people there had shooed him away when he had come to offer help during the plague.

He took a deep breath and knocked on the heavy wooden door. An elderly gentleman welcomed him in without asking his business. He offered Gabe a glass of water and motioned to his wife to bring one. Gabe began his speech, apologizing for not having told them sooner about the King being alive. At the mention of the King, the man laughed out loud.

"Alive? Did you miss his funeral? I thought the whole village was there. Do you think I'm a fool? Why would I believe a child telling a fairy tale? If that's all you've come for, you can go ahead and leave."

Gabe thanked them for the water and left without argument.

Gabe was relieved when he recognized Emily at the next farmhouse he entered. She and her husband remembered Gabe's kindness when their son, John, had been sick and were happy to welcome him in.

"Can I get you a glass of water?" Gabe declined, remembering the half-drunk glass he left at the last house.

"I have something I wanted to apologize for." Gabe looked with kindness at their confused faces. "I have known for more than three years that the King is alive. I have been meeting with the King on his hill and learning about his law. I have been teaching my sister and father about the King all these years, but I haven't told you about him before. I'm sorry that I have waited so long, but I would like to invite

77

you now to come to our home this evening to share a meal and to learn about the King and his law."

Gabe said it all in one breath and now practically gasped for air. For a moment, his audience sat stunned. Emily looked to her husband, who looked to Gabe. "We would be happy to come and learn more. We know that you are a good boy and wouldn't be playing a trick on us. If your father is listening to what you have to say, we are willing to as well."

"Thank you," Gabe said in relief. He shook their hands and went out the door. While there were a few homes that rejected him, there were many who wanted to believe Gabe because of his kindness and bravery during the plague.

Gabe eventually made it through the farmhouses along the stretch from the inn to the Square and turned back home. He had thought that the next day he would continue farther, that word of the King had only made it to the farmers, but as the farmers made it to the markets that day, news of the King being alive traveled with them.

Standing by the village well, Vulpine's senses were on high alert as he detected a change of tone in the harmony of the village. He was certain he discerned discord among the villagers. Phineas had made an announcement and not everyone was parroting his words. When they did, it was a beautiful melody to Vulpine. Now a sour note was written into the strain. Insistent on rooting it out, he directed his spies

78

to report on all village activity and discourse. By moonrise, he had his finger on the key. It was the King.

That evening two meetings were held. While the Brothers and Sons met at one of the member's homes, the farmers, some with wives, some with children, ventured over to the inn. Some felt a little foolish, some bubbled with anticipation, but all brought a gift of food to share with the others who had come to hear about the King.

Gabe, along with Angela and their father, welcomed the guests. Mother and Tabitha kept to the family quarters upstairs, but the rest shared a meal and listened to Gabe tell about his years at the King's feet. When he finished, they all stood under the golden glow of the lanterns overhead and sang the King's song.

The other meeting that night had a very different tone. "How could this have happened?" Vulpine fumed before his fellow secret society members. "Why is there talk of the King being alive? Who has the answers? How did this ugly rumor of the King's death being falsified get circulated?" A few snickered at the question, but Vulpine silenced them with one shot from his eyes. "These rumors must be squelched at once! For the peace and unity of the village!"

Chapter 10

"For the peace and unity of the village!" Vulpine was now ardently addressing the Assembly. "For the peace and unity of the village!" The members of the Assembly rallied around their leader. Phineas led the villagers in the same battle cry. "For the peace and unity of the village!"

Ironically, to accomplish this peace, Vulpine turned to General Writ. He issued orders that the General lead his troops up King's Hill. If someone was sitting on the throne, then he was an imposter and must be killed. "We cannot let an imposter disrupt the peace and unity of the village!"

Very early the next morning, a trumpeter rallied the troops to the square. There were several notable absentees, but roll was not called. The troops marched behind their subordinate leader toward the hill. Percy Katrid kept in line as he marched, wanting to see what Vulpine was up to.

At the base of the mountain, General Writ divided his troops into three squads. Two were to march up the right and left flanks; the third was to come from the front. They would converge at the summit when the signal was given. They were ordered to destroy nothing except any man found sitting on the throne. He was to be killed without hesitation.

Gabe, who had stopped on his way up the hill to wait and watch what was happening, shivered when he heard a rallying cry ring out from the troops. The village men were fearless, even though—or maybe because—they had never actually fought in battle before. They had trained but few weapons had been created for them. So while some were armed with swords and bows and arrows, even more were armed with pitchforks and knives. A team of ten had the unenviable task of transporting a cannon up the face of the hill.

The animals remained hidden as the squads progressed slowly up the unfamiliar terrain. At the edge of the pine forest, the troops awaited the signal to charge. First, the cannon, only to be used if they were ambushed at the peak, had to be in place. The men had rammed the charge down the cannon's barrel, rolled in the cannonball and placed the fuse. One man stood poised with a flint in his hand.

General Writ raised his saber. The signal. The charge. Men from all sides marched double time up the final ascent, brandishing their weapons and releasing guttural cries. Some relished the thought of piercing through the imposter and becoming a hero, perhaps a legend in the village. The prospect spurred them on.

Now the cave was in view. The cries grew louder, the men's animal instincts possessing them, enabling them to kill or be killed. The three squads converged at the summit, and in one great, climactic moment, everything fizzled. The throne was empty. The trees and streams and flowers and rocks were silent.

General Writ ordered a thorough search of the cave, but it was small and solid and no hiding places were found. Before all the adrenaline disappeared, Vulpine himself appeared. He had followed the troops at a safe distance but had been prepared for such an outcome.

"Men! Do not be disappointed! You are the great ones of this village!" Vulpine's grandiose words struck a chord with his audience. He had their attention and held it as he made his way toward the cave.

"This village has suffered greatly recently from the terrible sickness, and it is now suffering again from rumors that the old King is living and ruling from this empty spot. You bravely put yourselves in harm's way to defend the honor of the village. You stood for the truth and the truth prevailed today!" The men cheered.

"We can't allow the suffering to continue. The village needs a leader, a real leader who is strong enough to make firm decisions and to guide our village into the future. Not a distant king who never makes himself seen or heard." He paused and placed his hand on his heart.

"The village has suffered, as we all know. And the weak ones of the village have turned to these lies about the King as a way to comfort themselves. So I propose that in order to accommodate the weaker members of our village, we should give them a king. A true leader who will speak for all members of the village, one who understands the weak, but who is man enough to lead the strong." The members of the Brothers and Sons were listening intently for their cue. It had all been decided beforehand. "And who do you think is the only one able to fill this role with wisdom and dignity?"

It was time. "King Vulpine! King Vulpine!" The chant began among a dozen scattered men but was soon picked up by others. "King Vulpine! King Vulpine!"

Vulpine thrilled to hear his name exalted. He put on regal airs and glided toward the throne. Two men came after him, carrying a king's robe and a bronze scepter. They raised the blood-red robe, and Vulpine slipped his arms inside. He took up the scepter and thrust it skyward.

Gabe had remained at the hill's base anxiously waiting, plucking up shoots before they could bloom in all their golden glory. Watching for a sign of what was happening past the shield of the forest, he heard the men's voices steadily rising and falling like the call of a kingbird, but he couldn't fathom the meaning of the din. Percy Katrid understood all too well.

"King Vulpine! King Vulpine!" The men urged him on with their repetitious shout. He lifted his other hand, motioning for silence, and the men quieted. "Let the will of the people be accomplished!" He sat on the throne. Vulpine luxuriated in his rich surroundings. Percy took one look at Vulpine sitting there and spat on the ground.

The men of the village whooped and cheered. Then a new chant emerged from within their midst. "Long live King Vulpine!"

Phineas Tract knew all was going as planned. Now he was to head up the next phase. Standing on the far side of the mass of men, he called out, "Men, let us go into the village and announce the tremendously good news that King Vulpine has begun his reign!"

Vulpine remained behind, tended by servants. Phineas shepherded his herd back to the village where the chant was taken up again. "Long live King Vulpine!" They moved slowly through the streets. Curious women and children emerged from their homes, trying to understand what their senses were taking in. Once in the square, Phineas proclaimed the day a holiday and welcomed everyone to come in the evening for feasting and dancing.

The men scattered to spread the news and to relate all that had taken place that morning on the hill. Gabe's father, who had remained at home, was visited by Percy, their friendship deepened by their agreement over Vulpine.

Gabe returned home and paced around behind the inn, kicking at pebbles and deep in thought. He couldn't make any sense out of what was happening. He reviewed the facts. *They hadn't found the King. Where was he? Vulpine now is king. Says who? Everyone. Not me. Vulpine wants the King dead. But he can't find him. I don't know where he is either. Today was the first day in three and a half years I didn't pay a visit to the King.*

At the realization, he slumped into the dirt. He felt like that ten-year-old boy again, being bellowed at by Vulpine and wishing he would just go away. He picked up a stick and started doodling in the dirt. His heart flooded his eyes, and a tear rolled down his cheek. He let the tear tickle his chin. *What now? Where are you, King? How can I talk to you?* A thought came to him. If he couldn't physically sit at the King's feet and hear his words spoken to him, he could read his words in the Book of Law.

His countenance brightened, and he felt that again the King had somehow been responsible for lifting his heavy burden. He flew up the stairs to the family's quarters and found Angela had beaten him to it. Sitting with their great-grandfather's papers on her lap, she grinned at him and, as if reading his thoughts, handed him some sheets. "Do you know he's gone?" Gabe asked as he squatted next to her.

She shook her braids back and forth. "He's not. He's right here with us. His words are in his law and in our hearts. We'll sing his song and share his words. He promised to come back to the village one day. You'll see him again, and I'll see him too." Gabe remembered the last thing the King had said to him and clung to the words of encouragement— he wasn't alone and he would see the King again.

"We need to keep meeting with the others," Gabe said, having caught Angela's infectious enthusiasm. "We can't let this stop us. We know the truth. The truth hasn't changed. We need to keep telling others. They need to know that Vulpine is the imposter and the real King lives and reigns over our village."

Gabe sprang to his feet. "I'm going to tell everyone that we are still meeting tonight at the inn. We won't let anyone forget about the King."

Gabe wasn't the only busy one that afternoon. It seemed that half of the village women had fluttered about most of the day preparing for the party and were finally satisfied with their work as the sun began to set. Lanterns encircled the festivities, each lit as it hung in front of one of the shops lining the Square.

The women prattled on and on about their new king while a group of men gloated over their numerous kills. They had been sent to King's Hill that morning to hunt for the feast and had found an abundance of game. The children, dressed in their best, held hands and skipped and twirled to the music of their lighthearted laughter.

Phineas, standing on the steps of the Hall attracted everyone's attention. "In honor of our king, King Vulpine, let the festivities begin!" Cheers went up. Music played. The strings twanged. The brass trumpeted. The winds whistled. The percussion boomed. The people stamped and clapped and forgot all about their troubles.

They feasted on roasted bear, deer, pheasant and quail. They gorged on apricots, cantaloupe, plums, mushrooms, potatoes, squash, nuts and dates. They drank their fill until only good memories of the village and Vulpine swam in their heads.

After several hours of revelry, a hush came over the celebration. Vulpine had come down to them. An excited whisper passed like a wave to and fro, undulating through the gathering. Vulpine climbed the steps of the Hall, his robe carried by two men who carefully draped it over the steps for an impressive effect. Vulpine still carried the scepter and looked every part a king.

He raised his arms and addressed his subjects. "My good people, we have this day begun on a new course that will lead us into a prosperous tomorrow. I humbly accept your decision to make me your king and ruler supreme over the village. I will rule with gentleness over all who seek the peace and unity of our village and with an iron fist over all who seek its destruction."

The villagers cheered. "My first royal edict will be to open up King's Hill. Too long has it remained shrouded. I will not be a king like the other before me, completely removed from the life of the village. I will be among you and together we will make our village great!" More cheers and clapping and stomping and banging.

Phineas took the stage. "We have a special treat for you. The children's choir from our school will sing for us the village song, improved for the occasion." It was the same song that had replaced the King's after his funeral, but one line had been changed. "Our village" had been changed to "King Vulpine" so that the children pledged before their parents, "King Vulpine we will serve."

The tune was started again and the congregation sang the familiar melody, stirring up patriotism and pride in their hearts. With one voice they sang, "King Vulpine we will serve."

That evening at the inn, away from the festivities, there was a meal and singing and reading of the law. Percy Katrid was there for the first time and recounted the morning's events for the group. Gabe sensed there was something strange in the atmosphere, almost palpable, but only almost; he couldn't put his finger on it. Gabe's father, however, knew what it was—rebellion.

THE KING WILL MAKE A WAY

Chapter 11

From among the newly trained village men, Vulpine hired guards to serve him; most were stationed on King's Hill just past the edge of the forest. The trees traced their way across the hill, separating king from commoner. Vulpine had parceled out land along the forest green demarcation for Phineas Tract, General Writ and Assemblyman Tate, all of whom had devoted themselves to his service and had proven themselves useful to him. Assemblyman Stone was resentful to not be included in this elite treatment. His beady eyes leered at Vulpine through the smoke emitting from his pipe as he thought how he would make a much better ruler for the village.

But most of the villagers were thrilled with their new king. They were now free to use the forest and field for picnics and berry picking. Since Vulpine's coronation, hunting was allowed on the hill as well, and men were fashioning bows and arrows to catch their prey. Families began growing fat from their kill.

Vulpine continued to win the favor of the villagers. He took a small table made of gold from the throne room and had it melted down and made into little cubes of gold, which were given out to each family in the village. There was only one other thing Vulpine changed in the throne room. He had the wooden cabinet moved to the Assembly Hall. The single plate was carefully moved with it.

The cabinet became a tourist attraction among the villagers themselves. They loved to file past and find their homes on the intricately carved walls. They also loved Vulpine, praising his generosity and leadership—truly worshipping him.

No one was surprised when during the summer Vulpine decided the village song, in which villagers sang their pledge to serve Vulpine, would be sung daily in the square at midday. By fall, he had decided that attendance at the singing ceremony would be required on Sundays. Phineas announced the new law on a Saturday.

"King Vulpine has issued a new decree. From this day forward, each Sunday at midday, every villager, unless ill, must attend the singing ceremony in the square. Together we will proclaim our loyalty to King Vulpine. King Vulpine, in his wisdom, has decreed this to ensure the peace and unity of our village."

Gabe never followed Phineas down to the square. He heard about the new law that night at the meeting.

"What are we going to do?" Mrs. Bollix asked the group.

"We'll have to sing. It's the law." A short, wide man shared his opinion.

"I will not pledge to serve Vulpine." Percy Katrid was on his feet. "I refuse to call him king!"

"Can't we just go and not sing?" A timid woman offered her suggestion.

"That wouldn't feel right." Gabe's father stood by Percy. "Do you want to look like you're supporting Vulpine? It's time to take a stand."

"I don't—" Gabe saw his father's paternal glare meaning "this is not the time for you to be heard" and bit his lip.

Several men agreed and walked over to stand by Percy and Father.

Percy walked over to one of the tables and leaned his calloused hands on the oak slab. "This is only the beginning. Little by little he has changed our lives. He doesn't want just change though. He wants control. He's hungry for power. He wasn't satisfied with being head of the Assembly. He wanted all the power to himself. He made himself king. He has made it so he will never have to face an election. And he will get away with whatever he wishes, unless someone stops him. There is no longer any law in the village to use against him. Since he's put himself above the law, the only way to stop him is by force."

Many mumbled their agreement. Gabe retreated to the kitchen. Mother was rubbing salt between her fingers, raining it down on the simmering soup. "What's the matter? Not getting bored with King talk are you?" Gabe really wanted to talk to someone, but his mother wouldn't understand. He wandered out back. *At least Betty is a good listener.*

He stroked Betty's tan fur. "Everything was so perfect, Betty. Now I don't know. I wish I could go ask the King what was happening, what was right. They don't even want to hear me speak at the meeting." Betty mooed sympathetically. "They are listening to Percy Katrid, and he doesn't know anything about the King. He just doesn't like Vulpine. Vulpine is more important to him than the King. He doesn't care about the King. He's just using our meetings to gather support because he knows we don't like what Vulpine is doing." *Whining isn't helping. What am I supposed to do?*

The law. Gabe began reasoning to himself. *If the King were to rule, then we would be following his law. If they really want Vulpine out and the King in, then they should obey the King's law.* Gabe wandered up to the family quarters and found the stack of papers marked with his great-grandfather's ink scrawl. *Now where in these pages does it talk about all this?*

Gabe knew the King didn't want them to fight. All these years had passed, and the King had never encouraged a revolt against the village leaders. He just knew it wasn't the King's way to encourage his people to rebel against their leaders. But he couldn't prove it without finding it in the law. He knew the King's ways because he had sat at the King's feet and had learned straight from the King's mouth, but no one was listening to a kid right now. *I'm just a kid.* He tried to forget about that last thought, though he wasn't so good at forgetting. He'd been trying to forget for years about the time he fell into the well in the square because he had been showing off, trying to walk the cross bar where the bucket is tied.

Focus. King! His heart cried in desperation. *Where do I find your words about all this? They are going to go to war for your sake and you don't want them to.* He flipped through the pages of the law barely glancing down, despairing at the task. It was like searching for a star in the sky without knowing your constellations. You need the constellations to guide you, and Gabe needed the King. He tossed the papers onto the floor, and they glided to a standstill. Gabe held his head in his hands and closed his eyes.

He saw the King. He was on his throne, smiling. Gabe felt a little light-headed in his presence but was still in control of himself. He could hear part of what the King was saying. "The law is just and justice will prevail. Vengeance is mine. I am the only one able to rule with justice. No one else can see with the clarity that I am able to see from my throne above the whole village. I know the moves and motives of everyone in the village. Justice will be done, but justice cannot be delivered except by a pure hand." Gabe's eyes remained shut fast, but he could no longer see the King. He remembered that day. The King had taught him about justice and revenge. *Now to find those words...*

Gabe snatched up the top sheet and with the same momentum, propelled himself up onto his feet. He started doing a jig, hopping, leaping and kicking around the upper room. He had found it. *Had it been right there on top all this time?* Gabe didn't stop to ponder. He did a few more leaps and laughed, wondering what they were hearing down below.

He made it down the stairs in two bounds. From the kitchen, he barreled through the door so hard it bashed against the wall. He didn't slow until he had jumped with two feet and landed on a bench.

He didn't need to quiet everyone to get their attention. His grand entrance had left them speechless. He held up the aged paper and began to read:

"Vengeance belongs to the King. Do not take revenge, but trust the King to bring justice. Do not pay back evil with evil, but pay back evil with good. If someone slaps you on one cheek, turn and give him your other cheek. Love your neighbor and treat him as you want to be treated. Above all, love the one and only King. Serve him and obey his laws. This is your first and most important duty."

"This is the King's law." Gabe had stopped reading and was speaking unrehearsed words from his heart. "These are his own words that he gave us to live by. Percy Katrid would have you believe that we are to fight Vulpine to win back the throne for the King, but he doesn't know the King. I know him and now you know what he says about this. If you believe the King exists, then you better obey his law. If you don't believe, then go with Percy to your destruction."

As soon as he had finished speaking, reality smacked him in the face. He was standing taller than everyone else and telling adults what to do. He deflated like a balloon and flopped limply onto the bench, wanting only to slither under the table and hide.

Most were too flabbergasted to speak, but Percy was angry enough to let off steam, a teapot at full boil.

"Kid. You have no idea what you are talking about. We aren't playing here. We're talking people's lives. Vulpine isn't going to stop his rule by our being nice to him. We need to take action. Every minute delayed is another minute Vulpine's vice-like grip on the village tightens. I'm leaving this meeting. I will only be where the real men are. Anyone who wants to fight for freedom can follow me." To add emphasis, he trod heavily across the floor and exited the inn without looking back.

Several men left without further deliberation. Those with wives at their sides dragged them out the door too. Marcus Winsley stood up slowly, hat in hand. "I just want to do what's best for the village. This is my home." He looked down at his grown son sitting next to him. "My children's home. I can't let it all be taken away." He apologized and left after the others. His son followed.

Father turned his attention to Gabe. "You know I believe in the King, but Vulpine is restricting us so we can't even follow all of the King's laws if we wanted to. If Vulpine were gone, we could follow the King's ways. It's just never going to happen while Vulpine is ruling. Don't you think the King wants to sit on his throne again? He would want us to get Vulpine out of there. We need to do something. I just don't see any other way." Gabe's father walked out the door of his own inn.

It was Gabe's turn to be stunned. He felt like Betty had kicked and knocked the air out of him. He couldn't think of anything to say. Then he heard Angela's voice, strong and

97

steady like the tolling of the village bell so that everyone could hear its message.

"Vengeance belongs to the King. Do not...." Angela had picked up the yellowed, tattered paper and was reading as Gabe had done. When she came to the end, the lilting words of the King's song followed. Those remaining, men and women alike, some younger than Gabe, some shriveled with age, all stood and joined in the refrain. They sang their devotion to the King, the one true King. They sang the song that had been silenced on the hill.

Chapter 12

Percy led the way around the back of his home, the only light a single candle in a window. He pushed aside a couple of bales of hay which concealed the cellar entrance, and a well-fed rat scurried out of the way. For a moment, Father questioned his wisdom in following Percy into the dark with the small mob of angry men. Tobacco smoke startled his senses and unhinged his thoughts. He followed Percy down the steps into the cellar and left his doubts out in the cold, dark night where they could vanish with the warm morning light.

The smoke was curling from the lips of four men relaxing in arm chairs. A few dozen men filled the hideout. No one was talking. They were watching and waiting. The other dozen men with Percy felt like animals being shown to buyers at the market. All eyes were on them. They tried not to show fear—they were pretty sure the others would be able to smell it.

Percy broke the silence. "We need all the good men we can get. Tomorrow is the day. We'll see what Vulpine and each of us are made of. I'll let Assemblyman Stone bring everyone up to date with the details."

"Thank you." Stone put down his pipe and spoke from his seat. "I will say outright that you are the wisest men in our fine village. You have seen beyond the masks and lies and have discovered the truth for what it really is. I commend you all. The imposter Vulpine surely is cunning, but his arrogance has led him to believe he can control us with bribes and fancy words. He thinks too highly of his own power.

"I offer to you that this is his blind spot. With a precise blow, we can bring him down. He has already stripped the Assembly of its power. The four of us upright Assemblymen have not bowed to Vulpine. The majority have, however. They are greedy for money and power and despise virtue." Stone rose and began methodically pacing the length of the room. Every eye trailed him. His words were working their charm, building confidence in each of them that they were on the side of right. Doubts drifted away and disappeared with the tobacco smoke. Stone had attracted them to the lure and now was ready to hook them.

"You are the saviors of the village. You are standing for freedom instead of becoming servants to that imposter. You are the ones able to right this tremendous wrong committed against you and your families. Our village needs you to rescue it. Your children need you. Even those foolish enough to follow Vulpine need you. Look around. There are many able-bodied men here. We are not at a disadvantage.

"We know Vulpine's weakness, do we not? He doesn't think it is possible that he could lose control of such a large number of his subjects." He spat the word. "He won't see it coming. We will be victorious! Let me explain the plan." He took his seat, reclining again and grinning as if he were at a party and not a war counsel.

"Our spies tell us that in the morning Vulpine will condescend to be among the common folk," Stone mocked. "He wants to see for himself the results of his edict that everyone be at the village singing ceremony. Vulpine has kept silent as to what he intends to do to violators. That is one of the few unknowns we face. But I don't see it as a complication, as we don't intend to let him do a thing. Let me get back to the plan.

"While confident of our sources, we don't want to risk being caught unprepared, so we will cover King's Hill as well. Percy here will lead a dozen men up the hill early in the morning. They will go under the pretense of hunting. By late morning, they will be in position. Percy will lead the charge. He will give them more details when they are in the forest tomorrow morning. Percy, have you chosen which men you want to take with you?"

"I'll take the ones I brought with me tonight. I trust them with my life." The men who stood behind Percy were sure he had spoken the truth and their chests swelled.

"Very well. The remainder of you will be under the orders of Perkins and Howe. Perkins will hide a half dozen of his men behind the Assembly Hall. Another dozen will be inside, oohing and aahing over the architecture and that cabinet of theirs with the carving of the village." Stone was enthralled with his own cleverness.

"That leaves Howe. He and his men will be with those singing in the square. When Vulpine is announced, they will rush the Assembly Hall where Vulpine will be on the porch in front of his adoring crowd. Vulpine will be surrounded. Percy and Howe, divvy up your men."

There was a short burst of commotion as the men divided the troops between them. Stone was back on his feet and pacing again. As the men's energy focused again on him, he stopped behind his high-backed chair. Leaning into it, he gripped its faded brown leather.

"Men, your leaders have already discussed this next point, but I would like to know what you think. We are in this all together, are we not?" The rhetorical question only brought forth a few grunts. The grin was back on Stone's face. "What do you think? Should we make Vulpine surrender as our prisoner, or does the dastardly devil deserve to die?" Each word was spoken with more force than the one before. The crescendo climaxed with a war whoop from the men. "Kill him!" "Let him die!" Gabe's father was surprised by the sudden transformation of the men. They had become ravenous sharks, attacking when they smell blood. At the mention of Vulpine's name, the scent wafted through the air.

Vulpine had been watching the movements in the village. He considered the villagers pieces on a giant chess board. The pawns he didn't have any concern for, since their movements were easily manipulated. For now he would leave the bishops be and watch how the game progressed. He knew of their meetings at the inn and their disloyalty, but they were a bunch of weaklings: women, children and old men. Only a few straggly others joined them. There were the rooks, his guards; the queen, his devoted servants whom he could bid come at a moment's notice; and he, of course, was the king. That left the knights, those horses that fancied themselves special—the only pieces on a chess board allowed to jump over another. Vulpine was sure if they tried to maneuver over him, he would knock them down.

Saturday night Vulpine gathered to his throne his inner circle: Phineas Tract, General Writ and Assemblyman Tate, all members of the Brothers and Sons. "Word has spread that

I will be at the singing ceremony tomorrow in the square. From our information, it seems our rogues will try and attack me during the ceremony, using the Assembly Hall as the center of their attack. I will speak to each of you privately about your role. Phineas and Tate will be at the ceremony with several of the guards. Writ will be right here. Do not say a word to anyone until necessary. Just have all your men present and alert. I have tested you each and found you trustworthy, but even now I will not speak freely. Do not trust anyone until this rebellion has been thoroughly stamped out. But men, this is an exciting day dawning. We knew this had to come. It's part of the birth pains of any new government. The leaders of the rebellion speak of freedom, but they are hypocrites and really just seek after power for themselves."

Each man had a whispered session with Vulpine. Not one mentioned a thing to another as they stood in the blackness of the night.

THE KING WILL MAKE A WAY

Chapter 13

A hawk swept over the village. The sun hadn't peeked over the horizon yet, but light was beginning to fill the expanse of the sky. Farmers were tending to their animals. Babies cried for milk. Children rolled over and snuggled into their blankets. A long, thin black dog sniffed his way through the streets, searching for a discarded treat. A calico cat walked a fence rail. It was Sunday.

Gabe and Angela had slipped from bed when it was still dark. They sat with a candle beside them, casting both light and shadows on the words of the King's law. Reading those words was all they could think of to help them prepare. They felt as if they were headed into a dark tunnel with no light yet showing at the far end. They didn't know what the day would bring. They didn't know Percy's plans. They didn't know what Vulpine would do. They didn't know what would happen to people who didn't show up to sing in the square. People like them.

A jarring sound clashed with the early morning tranquility. Whack. Thwack. Tap. Tap. Tap. Whack. Thwack. A hammer pounded a code that echoed off King's Hill, delivering the message to the inn. What did it mean? Angela and Gabe wanted to know and raced each other down to the Square. Watching from afar, they crouched in the shadows of the Assembly Hall.

They couldn't make out what they were seeing, but it certainly was altering the appearance of the Square. Two men knelt on a wooden platform. What they were pounding on was lying flat. Shortly the workers stopped and together raised the first form.

One man leaned on the frame while the other started hammering again at its base. The wooden form had an upright post, shorter than the man holding it, and a cross bar making it look like a squat capital letter T. The beam across the top had three holes cut in it, one large in the middle, two smaller ones at either side.

Feeling that this was important, they patiently waited for the workmen to finish. The seconds felt like minutes and the minutes like hours, but they watched as the workmen secured another wooden frame to the platform. And another. And another. And another.

Gabe and Angela weren't sure what they were looking at but knew it was unlike anything they had seen before. An ominous feeling tied Gabe's stomach in knots. "Let's get out of here." Angela didn't need more. They wouldn't have run faster if a black bear had been chasing them. They tumbled into the inn and into their father.

"Where have you two been?"

"Down to the square. There are men constructing something. I don't know what it is." Gabe proceeded to describe it.

"They are a punishment for criminals," Father explained. "The neck fits in the larger hole and the wrists in the smaller holes. That top bar opens. The criminal is put in place and then the top is locked down. He has to stand out there all day in front of everyone. You're sure they built one of those down there?"

"They built five." Gabe delivered the bad news to his father.

Father looked down the road. "I'm going hunting this morning with Percy and some others. Tell Mother not to expect me home until evening." Father was distracted and left without saying goodbye.

After watching Father leave, Angela turned to Gabe. "Ten hours of hunting? What's going on?"

"They're using it as an excuse." Gabe fixed his gaze on King's Hill. "They will all be gathered with their weapons in hand. Maybe they are planning to attack Vulpine today. Maybe they just want to be prepared in case Vulpine does something drastic. Father hasn't said anything. I don't know Percy's plan, but we know he wants to fight." Gabe looked at Angela. He had to look up a little as she had sprouted before he had. "There's nothing we can do. Let's just act like it's any other day."

Angela opened her mouth to speak, but she closed it again seeing Gabe turn his back to her and head calmly into the kitchen. They set about doing their chores.

Brad Winsley finished up his own chores in the barn and struck out with his father. He had made them each a set of bow and arrows. Having bonded over target practice, Marcus was proud to have his son in step with him. They smiled at each other knowingly as Marcus patted the dagger in its sheath under his vest. Gabe's father strode up alongside them, but they didn't greet each other. Their pinpoint focus was at the top of the hill.

The dozen men arrived in installments—a few here, a few there—each disappearing into the pines and then reconnecting at their designated meeting point. Gabe's father reported what he had learned from his children. Then Percy laid out the plan.

"We'll spend some time this morning hunting in two groups. We'll keep close and maintain contact. We'll work our way up the hill throughout the morning. We will be all together at the upper edge of the forest on the left flank before midday. When we hear the bell stop ringing, we'll attack the guards. With Vulpine at the ceremony and expecting there might be trouble, there shouldn't be more than a few guards. We'll outnumber them and take them easily." Percy was feeling cocky.

"Then we can take turns sitting on the throne." He laughed out loud and put the men at ease, all but Gabe's father. He couldn't stop thinking about seeing his son standing in front of everyone the night before, reading from the King's law. For some reason, he couldn't remember the words.

Those same words permeated Gabe's mind. He replayed the night over and over, setting his jaw to hide the heartache each time he thought of his father leaving the meeting. *What is he doing now?*

Mother noticed Father's absence right away. Gabe gave Father's message with such sadness she couldn't help but feel nervous. She hummed to herself as she peeled apples to try and not think about it. She would just be glad that her children were there with her.

Angela was putting Tabitha's hair in braids, singing silly songs to escape her worries. When their mother called, they came promptly and sat at the table for breakfast. No one noticed if it was good or not. Mother jabbered on about the Griver's chickens running loose, about the size of the pumpkins at the market and how she had heard the Henkin's boy had almost set fire to his family's barn. If you had asked them afterwards, not even Mother could have told you what she had mentioned.

When the children pushed back their bench to rise from the table, she grabbed Gabe's arm. "Listen, I know we think differently on some things these days, but I am your mother, and I want what's best for you. I don't know what's going on, but I can feel in my bones it's no good. Your father has himself mixed up in a fine mess, I'm afraid. I'm so glad you two are not out with him. But later today, I will be in the square with Tabitha, obeying our king. I hope to see you there. Vulpine is our king," she repeated for emphasis.

"We won't be there, Mother," Gabe answered sullenly.

"Then don't go for King Vulpine. Go for the sake of the village," Mother begged.

"We don't serve the village either. We serve the King. We can't go to the square today. I know you don't understand. Punish us if you must, but we can't go."

110

"I wash my hands of it. I won't feel guilty for whatever becomes of it. This is your decision. You will take the consequences." Mother stomped out of the kitchen.

"What are we going to do?" Angela was the one searching for answers this time.

"I don't want to be around here. Let's go to King's Hill. It's the most peaceful place I know."

"Gabe, what about Father and the hunters?" Angela shook her head in disbelief at his suggestion.

"We'll stay near the bottom of the hill. I don't want to be here." His sad eyes stared at the door where their mother had just left the room.

"All right, let me say goodbye to Tabitha, and I'll be ready."

In the forest, Gabe and Angela made a nest of pine needles for a place to wait out the morning. Their father, Percy Katrid, and almost a dozen other rebels were gathering at their meeting point and inching their way to the uppermost edge of the forest, where General Writ and his men guarded the throne room.

Nearly twenty rebels were in the square, hidden among the waiting crowd, while the rest were either behind or inside the Assembly Hall. Phineas was on the steps of the Hall, speaking with the villagers. Vulpine was just inside the Hall doors, waiting to be announced. His guards were stationed at intervals around the square, each standing in front of a shop with a lantern hanging out front—the lanterns had been lit by order of Vulpine.

The midday sun continued on its arc, rising to the highest point in the sky.

THE KING WILL MAKE A WAY

Chapter 14

Phineas motioned to the boy who rang the bell to stop pulling the rope and smiled broadly at his audience, enjoying the clear, still day. Tabitha whined, asking when the music would start. She was shushed. The restless rebels shifted their feet and itched at their pockets. The sun reached its full potential.

The doors of the Hall were opened with flair as Phineas made his introduction, "Our great leader, his royal majesty, King Vulpine!"

****

Gabe's father stormed out of the forest following Percy. They had spied just two guards in front of the throne room and were full of confidence. The two Winsley men ran across to their position and fired arrows at the guards. One guard was struck but not killed. As the arrow hit its target, the hill shook with a deafening boom.

"What was that?" Angela's voice quivered.

"I don't know, but I'm going to see. What if Father's in trouble?"

Angela caught his sleeve. "Gabe, no. If you go up there, they will think you are part of the rebellion. We can't let that happen." Gabe shook himself loose, but stayed.

****

The rebels rushed forward as one toward Vulpine. Their formation stretched clear across the front of the Assembly Hall. They leapt up the stairs of the Hall and muscled everyone standing there into the building. Phineas had jumped to safety, but Vulpine was trapped in the middle of the mob.

The crowd panicked. Shrieks and cries came from the women and children, angry shouts from the men. Gabe's mother dragged Tabitha into the glass blower's shop to hide from the chaos. She didn't notice the lantern was gone from out front.

****

Gabe's father was knocked backwards, hitting his head hard. His comrade had fallen into him, crushed under a cannonball.   From inside the throne room, armed men emerged, a swarm of angry bees ready to sting. The Winsleys ran into the cover of the forest and didn't stop running, abandoning their weapons along the way. Percy swatted at the first bee which stung him, slicing at his arm, but these bees didn't die after they stung—they fought on. Percy was absorbed with the fight, his sword clanging against another's. The others were valiant at his side, all equally engrossed. They were outnumbered though, and each fell as a second or third guard surrounded him. Noticing Gabe's father on the ground, one of Vulpine's guards pierced his side with a sword.

Soon nothing moved other than Vulpine's guards. Several were being bandaged, but all had survived. General Writ congratulated his men as he surveyed the still landscape. "Toss the bodies over there. Leave them for the animals, a thank you for keeping our secret." General Writ thought he was witty and chuckled. The bodies were heaped by the edge of the forest. "A good day's work, men. A good rain should take care of the rest. You have my permission to take leave for the remainder of the day."

****

"Fire!" One of the rebels was the first to sound the alarm. Vulpine's guards had taken the lanterns, and some tossed them in through the windows of the Hall while others torched the porch. The fire raged on all sides, climbing the four walls of the Assembly Hall. The wood crackled. The men inside shouted. In the glass shop, Mother crumbled to the floor and rocked Tabitha against her chest.

115

The rebels from behind the Hall formed a bucket brigade. They were promptly arrested by Vulpine's guards. Other villagers took their place, passing a bucket back and forth, hand to hand, from the well to the fire. Still more brought containers, sending water onto the thirsty flames, which licked up the water as soon as it was poured out. The still air aided the firefighters; the fire never spread beyond its target—a bull's-eye.

Inside the Assembly Hall, the wooden cabinet with its intricately carved map of the village ignited. The flames snaked their way through the carving of the village, consuming it as it went: the Assembly Hall, the school house, the shops, barns, homes, farmland, the inn. The cabinet collapsed in ashes before the fire destroyed the image of King's Hill. Outside, the pillars adorning the front entrance snapped and crashed onto their foundation. There were no more cries from within. Outside, women wept and screamed and their frightened children imitated them. The firefighters carried on their work, passing buckets, vases and jugs—hand to hand, hand to hand.

****

Gabe and Angela ducked into their pine tree fort when they heard footsteps. Gabe spotted Brad and Marcus Winsley darting across their line of sight. "Did they go with Father this morning?" Angela whispered into Gabe's ear. He nodded

116

and whispered back, "I think so." Angela hated not knowing what was happening. They strained to hear what they could, but they weren't getting many clues.

It didn't seem long before they heard more footsteps coming down the mountain. These footsteps were very different though, unhurried and accompanied by talking, even laughing. Members of Vulpine's guard breezed past. Angela was happy she was closeted away behind their barricade of needles.

Gabe lay down flat on his back and stared up into the tangle of branches. "Gabe? Gabe?" He wasn't answering. He was wondering if he could see where the tip of the tree speared the sky. He wondered if a low-lying cloud could feel the pierce of the pine needles. He wondered what it felt like to be pierced through with a dagger, a sword. He wondered how his father had felt before he died. "Gabe? Gabe?"

"Don't you understand? No one else is coming down the mountain. Father is dead."

"Don't say that, Gabe." Angela's head started to swirl. "Maybe he escaped. Maybe he's hiding on the hill somewhere." Angela was desperately searching for an alternative explanation.

"Those guards weren't looking for people hiding in the woods, Angela."

Angela's world went tumbling, spinning. She was weak and dizzy. She grabbed hold of the dirt with both hands to try and hold on. She couldn't see straight. She felt like she couldn't breathe.

"Angela? Angela?" She had fainted, and Gabe was gently touching her cheek. "Angela? Angela?" Her eyelids fluttered. They cracked open and pinched shut. She took a deep breath. Her eyes opened and stared up at the wooden ladder. She wondered what she could see if she climbed limb by limb up the rungs to its top. She wondered if she would be able to see Father from up there. She wondered if she would see him lying on the ground, dead.

Gabe lay back down in their pine needle nest, and together they wondered.

Chapter 15

Gabe was dozing and Angela was singing softly to herself when a sparrow alighted on Gabe's hand. Gabe twitched and sat up with a start. The bird didn't budge. Angela propped herself up on her elbows. "I thought you might sleep all—" She caught sight of the bird on Gabe's hand, and whispered, "How long has that been there?"

"It just landed, but it doesn't seem to want to go anywhere."

Gabe wasn't quite right about that. The bird pecked gently at Gabe's wrist.

"What do I do, Angela?"

"Gabe, remember your first trip up King's Hill?"

"Yes, so? Help Angela, it's pecking me!"

"Gabe; the toad, the deer! This is not a normal bird. It should be scared of you instead of you being scared of it. Do you think the King sent him?"

119

"I do. You're right." Gabe spoke quietly, as if afraid his voice would startle the bird and scare it away. "Angela, maybe this means Father is okay." The sparrow stopped pecking as if it knew its message had been understood. Immediately, it flew up to a branch and then out of the pine tree fort. "I guess we'd better follow him," Gabe said as he scrambled to his feet and ducked out of the hiding place.

The sparrow flitted from limb to limb, tree to tree. Gabe and Angela floated along after it. Their heartache had been lifted from them. That's how Gabe knew for sure the King was there, somewhere. *Are we about to see the King?* They both tingled with excitement at the thought. They wore bright smiles and almost laughed as they climbed. They refreshed themselves slurping cool, clean water from a stream. They nearly skipped along after the sparrow, their hearts suddenly so light. Angela looked at Gabe with sparkling, dancing eyes. Then she looked around to find the sparrow and screamed in horror.

Shaking, stammering, she dropped to her knees and covered her face with her hands. Gabe froze in dismay. An icy cold shot down his spine. *Whatever made her scream is behind me right now.* He wanted to bolt, hide, anything but turn and see what had brought his sister to hysteria. He had that ten-year-old feeling again. *Be a man, Gabe.* The self-pep

120

talk was short and to the point. He was the man here now, the only one his sister could count on.

Muscle by muscle, he slowly turned. First, his knees swiveled. Then his hips. Next his torso. Shoulders. *Be a man, Gabe.* As his neck inched his head around the bend, his eyes squinted closed. *Be a man, Gabe.* He lifted his lashes to peek, pulling in his shoulders, flinching at the air.

He saw. Everything drooped. His eyes relaxed and opened. His jaw hung loose. His arms weighed down his shoulders. He, too, sank to his knees. It was the pile of discarded bodies. The rebels crushed under Vulpine's iron fist.

The sparrow had landed on the mound. Gabe didn't understand all that he was feeling as he looked at the pile. The tumult of emotion inside of him brewed and boiled over, spewing out at the innocent sparrow. "Why did you bring us here?" He screamed it as loud as he could, his face crimson. "I don't want to be here. I don't want to see this! Get away from us! Go!"

Despair circled Gabe like a vulture, taunting, laughing. "He's dead. He's dead. They're all dead. Lifeless bodies left for the birds. You might as well join them. Vulpine will be after you next." Gabe pounded the ground, sure he was going mad. The sparrow landed in front of him then lifted off again and back to the stack of bodies.

121

"I said go!" Gabe grabbed up a stone and heaved it at the bird. The sparrow escaped, and the stone landed with a moan.

A moan? "Angela, someone's still alive!"

She picked up her head. "What?"

"Didn't you hear that? Someone moaned. Someone's alive."

"Alive?" Angela was shaking her head, her body still trembling too much to move. "Gabe, I can't. I can't go over there. Don't make me go over there." The thought of those bodies sent a new ripple of tremors through her.

"Okay. Okay. It's okay. You don't have to do anything. I'll do it. It's okay." The sight of his sister so frail unnerved him.

Be a man, Gabe. He drew in a quick breath and held it as he launched out toward the pile. He was there in four long strides. Standing there close to it, he didn't see a pile—he saw men. Familiar faces with blank stares. He vomited. Another moan emitted from one of the men.

"Father?" The word slipped out. *Could it be him?* As he made his way around them, his eyes scanned the men frantically until they rested on his father's face. Gabe moved over to him and knelt gently by his head. "I'm here, Father. It's okay." His father let out a gasp of air that carried Gabe's name.

Gabe exhaled, and with the release his tears flowed. The dam had broken and everything he had felt and experienced that day came flooding out. He cried for his father. He cried for the rebellion. He cried over thinking his father was dead. He cried knowing he still might die. He cried for his mother and Tabitha in the Square. He cried for the terror Angela went through. He cried for the King.

Finally, Gabe's river of tears ran dry. It had washed away all his strength. He was drained, empty. "Father, I don't know what to do. I don't know how I could possibly help you." The sparrow returned and landed on his father's hand. It flitted up and then returned to rest on his father's hand. Again and again.

"You want to lead my father somewhere?" Gabe was too worn to concern himself over talking to an animal. "He can't even move!" Despair started cackling in his ear.

Angela thought of the King and the tremors stilled. "The King." Angela's voice broke Despair's spell.

Gabe shivered and shook off his enemy. "What? The King?"

"Gabe, the King is here. I don't know where, but he is here. There's no doubt he sent that bird to lead us to Father." Her voice broke off at his name. She hadn't gotten up the nerve to go look at him, but she called to him now. "Father,

I'm here with Gabe. You're going to be fine. We're going to take care of you. I love you!" She grew quiet and reflective.

"Angela, the King? I don't know what you're thinking yet."

"Sorry. The sparrow led us to Father. We know the King must have sent him. That bird isn't that smart or that caring on his own. So, somehow the King knows what's going on. He sees us somehow. If that sparrow wants to lead Father somewhere, then it's the King wanting to lead him somewhere."

"Angela, I believe the King sent the sparrow. I truly, truly do." He came next to her and sat down beside her. Holding her arm, he leaned into her ear. "Father can't even speak. He has no strength, barely any life in him. He can't move or even be moved."

"Gabe, listen. Think. If the King wants us to move Father, then he will make a way. He has to. He always has made a way."

The memories flashed before his eyes. The thousand times he slipped past the guard. The nightmare before the hailstorm. The inn and his family kept from harm. The words and boldness to speak out. The guilt removed and burdens lifted.

"He always makes a way. You're right. There's a way here. He's made a way somehow."

"Gabe!" A weak voice called to him. He jumped to his feet and ran to his father's side. "I can do it. Help me up." Gabe and his father both winced as Gabe lifted Father to help him sit, then stand.

Angela came along Father's right side. Gabe held him up on his left. One step. Two steps. Three steps. Four steps. They had hobbled about a foot's length. Their father was breathing like he had just finished a marathon. Gabe looked at Angela and shook his head.

Angela's face lit up. With her chin, she pointed to beyond Gabe. "The King!" He swung around, longing to see the King again! But it wasn't the King. A small but sturdy horse was coming their way. The golden mare walked slowly with her head held high as if in a royal parade. Her hair was a white diamond between her eyes, adding to her majestic airs.

Gabe swallowed down his longing for the King and explained to his father that the horse had come to carry him down the mountain. Before they could worry about how he was to mount her, she lay down. They helped their father onto her back and laid him down against her mane. She lifted him effortlessly, and they began their descent. Before they reached the road home, while still under the cover of the pines, they heard someone walking past. Gabe peeked through the branches and saw Phineas Tract heading up the hill—whistling a happy tune.

Chapter 16

Mother stumbled back a bit when she first saw Father—the sight was awful but the smell was worse. Spending part of the day among corpses brought home an unwelcome perfume. Mother regained her composure and managed to strip and bathe her loved one, getting a glimpse of where the sword had pierced his side. The children helped her get him settled comfortably in bed. He smiled faintly and slept.

Back in the kitchen, Mother dished up stew for all of them. Tabitha was in bed already, exhausted by the trauma of the day. Mother listened to the children's story, and then she shared her own. Gabe remembered seeing smoke, but he had been too consumed with himself to stop and consider what it had meant.

"I want to go see what's happening in the Square." Gabe was resolute. "If the fire is still going, maybe I can help. I need to see if everyone's been killed but Father. And Vulpine, did he die in the fire?"

Mother shook her head. "I don't see how anyone who had been inside could have survived."

"Mother, do you want me to stay with you?" Angela asked. Relief swept across her mother's face. "All right, I'll stay and help you."

"You don't need to help. Just stay here with me. My heart can't take any more separation today. Gabe, you stay away from any trouble. It'll be dark in an hour. Please try and be home."

"Yes, Mother."

Gabe was in the square in minutes. The fire was down to embers. The Assembly Hall had been reduced to ashes. The smell of fire usually brought cozy images of warm milk and porridge, but this smell was choking, nauseating, flesh and bone cooked into the ashy soup stirring before him as embers popped. The King's pearl plate sat in the ashes, the only thing that had escaped the fire other than the thick black smoke which billowed up into the sky.

Finally taking a good look around the square, he spotted the wooden frames. He had forgotten about them, a year's worth of events had taken place since the day had begun. He shuffled across to the platform at the other end with only the empty market stalls behind it and saw that the wooden frames had been filled just as Father had described. Heads and hands hung out of the three holes in each frame. One other man was bound hand and foot and tied to one of the posts. Six men had been arrested.

Gabe searched the grounds, littered during the earlier bedlam. He found a bowl of sorts and filled it with water from the well to give each man a drink, returning to the well when the bowl was emptied. None of the men spoke except for murmured thanks. As he tipped the bowl to the last man's lips, a rock stung him in the back.

"Ow!" He spun around. A white haired woman scowled at him.

"Leave them to die!" she hissed. "One of them your old man or are you one of them? Maybe you deserve to die too!" She grabbed up the closest thing to her and hurled it at him. He ducked. It had been a vase used earlier by the bucket brigade and then abandoned. Now it was shards. Another casualty.

"I don't know them!" He spoke forcefully to the old woman and surprised himself. "I'm not a rebel either. I serve the King, the one true King. But there has been enough death today. I don't want to see another man die." He was intensely earnest. The woman spat at him then backed away.

Gabe sat on the edge of the platform. *What now?*

"Who are you?"

Gabe turned around but couldn't tell which of the men had asked. All of their heads hung weighted with defeat.

"No one. I just wanted to help you."

"Why? Who are you?" The middle-aged man heaved his head up to see the boy. After a glimpse it flopped back down like week-old parsley, his long, unkempt hair covering his face.

"I'm a servant of the King."

"If you serve Vulpine, why are you helping us?" There wasn't any anger in his voice; no fight was left in him. He just thought it dubious that a servant of the king would help them.

"No, I serve the one true King. Vulpine may sit on the throne up on the hill, but he is not the King. He does not really rule us. I know the true King, and I will serve him until I die. You weren't serving him by fighting today. You were serving yourselves and maybe Percy Katrid and the others, but not the King. I brought you water because I serve the King."

"My name is Caleb. It's nice to meet you, servant of the King. Thanks for the water."

"If you are still here tomorrow night, I will try and come back to give you another drink." Gabe slipped off the platform and headed home.

When Gabe entered the inn, he was surprised to see people gathered—more than the night before. Everyone was looking to him.

He spoke fervently about the King, his law, his love, his return one day. He urged them to submit to the village leaders except when it would require them to break the King's law. He reminded them that the two most important laws were to love and serve the King and to love and serve each other.

"There must never again be fighting. It will not accomplish our goal." His mind flashed wildly. *Our goal? What is our goal?* "Our goal is to see the King not only sitting on the throne but honored by everyone in the village. The King has been away from the village for decades, but he has never tried to force his way in. He wants the villagers to seek him, to come to him, to learn from him. We need to show people the King. We need to get them to believe he is real and worthy of our honor and obedience. We can show them by our love for each other and by our love for our enemies."

"Love for our enemies! My husband was burned alive today by Vulpine's men. My only comfort is that devil burned with him!" Fire was in her eyes and hate was in her voice. Her hands were trembling. "Why should I love those men? Why would I serve a King who loves those hateful men?"

"We don't have to love them like we love our brothers. But we have to treat them like we would want to be treated. It

130

means if one of them is dying of thirst, we don't drag him out into the hot sun; we give him a drink of water. It means we welcome them into our meeting if they begin to follow the King. Please, no more hate. No more fighting. Today's tragedy should be enough for anyone to learn that lesson."

Gabe looked at Angela. She read from the King's law and led everyone in singing the King's song. They sang it over and over. The words washed away their burdens and fears. Tears cascaded from the woman's eyes, putting out the fire they had contained just minutes before.

Everyone slept deeply that night, exhaustion a friend of sleep. Gabe dreamed the King had returned. All the villagers knelt before him as he stood on a platform in the Square. Gabe was standing next to him, wearing brilliant white. Then the people started shouting, "The King is alive! The King is alive!" He smiled and stirred.

"Gabe, what is it? Gabe, are you awake?" Angela leaned over Gabe trying to get him up. "Gabe, what are they saying? What's going on?"

Gabe returned to consciousness, still remembering his dream. Or was he still dreaming? It was only the cusp of dawn, but the village bell was tolling. A crier was galloping on horseback through the streets calling out. Turning around past the inn, the rider's words rang out clearly as he rode back. "The king is alive! The king is alive! Everyone to the Square!"

Gabe and Angela stared dumbly at each other until Mother shooed them out of bed. "Go find out what's going on! I'll stay home with Father. And look, Tabitha is sleeping right through it as usual. I couldn't wake that child if I dropped her on her head."

Angela and Gabe pulled on clothes. Gabe hopped out the door as his right leg hadn't yet found the end of its tunnel. They were out of the inn before Gabe had even spoken a word. All along the road, doors were opening as bewildered people stepped out of their homes. Gabe told Angela about his dream.

"Do you think it could really be him?" Angela asked, afraid to get her hopes up.

"I...I don't know. My dream about the storm happened, right?" *Please let it be you, King.* "Let's hurry." They were off again, just like the day before.

On the far side of the Square with the sun rising before them, the men, limp on their wooden hangers, cast long shadows. Inside the bell tower, a young boy tugged a tattered rope to rock the bell, and with each rock back, the bell tugged at the boy.

As the villagers arrived in the Square, they gathered in front of the platform. Everyone was trying to decipher the message of the crier. They were bursting with curiosity. Bewilderment gave way to excitement. Gabe's heart ached with the anticipation.

General Writ and numerous guards stood off to the side, and as Phineas stepped up onto the platform, the bell quieted. The crowd was as silent and still as those mornings when ice has glassed over the world.

He simply said, "May I present to you, your king!" Angela squeezed Gabe's hand. *Could it be?*

Chapter 16

"King Vulpine!" At Vulpine's name, the crowd didn't cheer or applaud. If everyone had been still and silent before, they were now frozen. No one dared do anything that might break the spell of those words. Then in a dramatic, magical moment, Vulpine emerged from among the guards. He leapt onto the platform. Hundreds of icebergs thawed.

One woman screamed. Another fainted. One man just started laughing hysterically. The baffled villagers started asking each other questions all at once. Phineas decided to help the dumbfounded commoners by shouting, "Long live King Vulpine!" The guards and the members of the Brothers and Sons joined in. "Long live King Vulpine!" Scattered groups took up the chant. "Long live King Vulpine!" The words picked up strength in numbers and in volume. And for the second time in twenty-four hours, Gabe vomited.

"Let's go home," Angela said as she took Gabe's arm and led him through the crowd. They walked past the ash heap,

134

out of the square and headed home. *How could he have escaped?* Without discussion, they slipped into the inn and back into bed.

Scarcely an hour passed before their mother shook them awake. "You have guests" was all she would say. She pulled open the curtain and unlatched the window only to shut it again, muttering something about a draft.

Downstairs in the dining hall, people had been arriving, but they were more family than guests. "Welcome everyone! No, no, it's fine to come now." Angela was a gracious host. "We don't always need to wait for nightfall. Please, come, sit down." People from their nightly meetings had come straight from the Square. Too much had happened to digest alone.

Gabe and Angela learned what had happened after they left the unveiling of Vulpine that morning. Winnie Goss shared the story with them.

"You were there at first, so you know what it looked like with everyone there crazy over Vulpine just showing up after we all thought he was dead." She struggled with a pin in her pepper black hair, which had noticeably begun turning salty. "He gets everyone yelling, 'Long live King Vulpine!' except those of us who were happy when we thought he was dead. Well, I did see some folks shouting along with them that I've also seen right here in this inn." Her plump fingers fiddled with the collar on her pale blue frock.

135

"Well, when all the commotion settles down, Vulpine doesn't even explain what happened—how he's alive—just starts talking about how he had fulfilled his promise to defend the peace and unity of the village. He told everyone it wouldn't happen again because the rebels were either killed or taught the 'invaluable lesson'"— she did her best impersonation of Vulpine —"that he knew everything that was going on and would always be one step ahead of anything the rebels tried. Then he had everyone sing that song. And you know who was singing? Those Winsley boys, father and son, just singing away. I left though, and I don't care who saw me. It wasn't law we sing today."

"I can tell you what happened after that. Do you recognize me?" He was addressing Gabe. Gabe squinted, trying to put the memory in focus.

"Caleb! You're free! Is that what happened next?"

Caleb smiled and rubbed his wrists. "I'm free. Vulpine had us freed. He told everyone it was to show his desire to keep the village united. He said he was sure we were convinced now by his 'miraculous reappearance,'"— it was Caleb's turn to try to imitate the baritone —"that he was the only king or something. All right, maybe I wasn't paying close attention. But I know that I'm free."

Gabe had one more question for Caleb. "How did you find me here?"

136

"I asked around about a boy who would offer a drink to a stranger." Caleb laughed. "It was pretty easy to find you."

Gabe only shrugged in response.

After the meal, Gabe took again to the bench and told everyone about his years at the King's feet. With tears in his eyes and a catch in his throat, he told them of the King's love and pleaded with them to follow the King's law. Angela read to everyone from the Book of Law and led the singing of the King's song.

As the others left, Caleb sidestepped over to Gabe. "I listened to you today, and I believe you. I believe you about the King. And I was wondering, how I can get to know him like you do."

"You can learn his words in the Book of Law. They will teach you who the King is. And by coming and being here with me and the others, you can feel what it's like to sit with the King and be loved. Most of the people here have dedicated themselves to following the King."

"I would really like to follow the King. How can I start reading the law book?"

Gabe felt foolish. *Why didn't I realize before this moment that I have the only copy of the law? We need to get it to everyone.* He gave a few pages to Caleb to start copying, and he and Angela worked on copying pages into the night.

At the next meeting, everyone was given a page, golden with age, to take home and copy as many times as they could. Every day they traded pages and went home and made more copies. In a month, they each had their own copy of the King's law and copies to share with others.

Now Gabe wasn't the only one teaching others the King's law. Everyone became a servant of the King, taking the King's law to their families and neighbors, and more and more people joined their meetings. Mrs. Bollix started teaching the King's law to her brother-in-law. She visited his family often to tell them what she was learning. He listened out of curiosity at first but eventually became interested in reading the King's law for himself. Mrs. Bollix was ready with a copy. Soon he was attending meetings at the inn.

Gabe and Angela started visiting Caleb and his wife and children daily. As a family, they studied the King's law eagerly. His five children, ranging from little to big, all learned the King's laws. Soon Caleb started meetings in his home for his relatives and close neighbors.

Sundays came and went and the servants of the King, as those at the meetings started calling themselves, stayed home from the singing ceremony, keeping quiet and hidden around midday. No one seemed to notice or mind—or, so they thought.

Vulpine had been watching those bishops to see what their next move would be. He knew they had mostly kept to themselves, but as the snow and ice enveloped the village, he noticed things heating up. The servants had begun teaching their neighbors about the King. Thirty servants became one hundred.

The quiet, straggly bishops were strengthening and getting louder. Vulpine wasn't blind or deaf to it. He knew how to take care of them. He would just need to pull on his iron glove.

THE KING WILL MAKE A WAY

Chapter 18

Another Sunday morning dawned. Caleb, having wanted to be alone, was on King's Hill reading the King's Book of Law. Angela and Gabe were sitting by a candle, wrapped in blankets, doing the same. They were preparing again. For what they didn't know, except that there had been rumors that Vulpine would make arrests.

Mornings started later in the winter, and by the time Betty had been cared for, the water fetched, the wash hung, the wood chopped and breakfast eaten, it was nearly noon. The children went upstairs to the family quarters. Father still spent his days in bed, but he could sit propped up for a short time. Angela brought him food while Gabe read to him from the King's law. Father had learned while lying almost dead on the hill that he should always listen to Gabe when he spoke the King's words.

The bell in the Square rang its chorus, its chime slipping easily over the icy fields through the bare branches of the trees and into the inn. Gabe and Angela tried not to be nervous, but they both stiffened at the sound. When the bell sang its last note, to those inside the inn, outside seemed lifeless. From their vantage point, the village seemed vacant, like the inn in the dead of winter.

"It feels like the day of the hailstorm," Angela said, standing at the window. "We kept watching and waiting, and then it sprung at us all of a sudden. Everything is so quiet and calm out there. I'm anxious though. I keep expecting something to happen." And then it did.

Coming at a quick pace down the snowy path from King's Hill came six of Vulpine's guards. Behind them was a horse-drawn cart with a cage built on top of it. Angela described it to her father. Gabe didn't wait to hear the description and darted to the window.

Closer and closer they trotted until they turned toward the inn. "They're coming here." Gabe catapulted himself out of the room.

Their pounding shook the door as the guards demanded it be opened. Gabe was there to obey the order.

"Sirs, welcome." He tried to act casual.

"We are under orders to arrest everyone not attending the singing ceremony today. You'll have to come with us. Is there anyone else at home?"

"Yes, my sister and I are here caring for our father. He's upstairs in his bed. Would you like to see them?"

"Take us."

Gabe led four of the guards up the stairs to the family quarters. Angela had heard them and sat by Father's bedside, wiping his face. He did his best to look miserable.

"They're just kids and the sick one. The law says you can stay home if you aren't well. Forget them."

Never before had Gabe been so thankful for his slight build. He was trying hard not to breathe, willing himself to be invisible. *Yes, just leave us here.*

"Come on." The guards found their own way out. Gabe didn't let out his breath until he heard the cart wheels in the snow. Angela was already at the window and flung it open.

"Gabe, quick! Look in the cage!"

Gabe hustled to the window. "Caleb!" Without thinking, he called out his name. Caleb heard, looked up at the window and smiled.

In dismay, Angela slumped to the floor. "What's happening out there?"

Gabe shut the window and without turning his gaze from the foggy pane, he started singing. Angela and Father added their soprano and bass, creating a memorable harmony with Gabe's tenor. He finally turned and looked at the others. "A beacon leading us out of our darkest night," he sang, repeating the line again. "When the King wrote the song, he was talking about this. Right now. Except we're not coming out of the darkest night, we're about to go into it. We can't forget the King. He's the one who will lead us out. We need to go tell Caleb." Then he added, "And any others."

There were others. The guards had swept through the whole village, house to house, arresting those who had defied Vulpine's mandate. The guards were shocked as they made their arrests. No one fought their captivity; some had even turned themselves in. Apart from the servants of the King, no one had defied Vulpine since the fatal attempt at rebellion. Even Assemblyman Stone was heard wishing Vulpine a long and illustrious reign.

The arrested servants were thrown into the village prison, one almost entirely dark and bare room. They were given bread and water and a bucket for a chamber pot that they were all expected to share. Men and women together were crammed into the stone room with nothing to sit or to lie on except the cold dirt floor. When the door was closed, there was no source of light except for the sliver at the bottom of the door.

Five men were chosen from their number to set an example for the others. They were locked into the wooden frames in the Square. The orders: the locks were not to be opened until the men were dead. That evening, the five men sang the King's song while the sun set behind them.

Gabe heard the news and after dark, took food and water to the captives in the square. Caleb was not one of them this time. With whispered encouragement, he helped them take bites of bread and cheese and sips of water. Before the sun came up again, Gabe had turned fifteen.

The next three days were unusually warm and pleasant. The snow and ice melted, and everyone who was able was outdoors. Angela even moved Father's bed next to the window. For the next two nights, Gabe tiptoed to the platform with a basket of food. The men were hungry, not only for food but for the King's words. Gabe fed them both. Each night, he slipped away promising to do whatever he could to come back again.

The third day, Vulpine conferred with his inner circle. "Someone's been feeding them. They should be wilted by now. They look happy!" The word "happy" had never before been spoken with such venom. He struck the golden arm of his throne, making his hand throb and him all the more livid. "Call the villagers to the Square. Let's be done with them."

The bell summoned the villagers, who hurried to see what was happening. Vulpine was on the platform, smiling, but his eyes were full of malice. He opened his arms wide to address the villagers.

"My loyal subjects, I come to you asking for your help. Together we will bring about our vision of peace and unity in our beloved village. But we must act together, united. Here behind me on this platform are five hideous creatures. They are disloyal, disobedient, a threat to the crown and to the village. To show your loyalty to the village, I ask you each to take a part in the destruction of these loathsome characters. Do what you will to them until they are all dead. That is your duty to the crown and to the village."

Vulpine stepped down quickly from the platform and concealed himself among his guards and officials. Phineas and Assemblyman Tate stood among them. At first, no one moved, unsure of what had just been asked of them. Then suddenly, a roar erupted from within the assembled crowd. A man rushed the platform and with a bound was on top of it. In an instant, he started boxing the face of one of the servants of the King, who was utterly helpless to defend himself.

The sight egged on others. More climbed onto the platform for their turn. They punched, stabbed, kicked, spat, yanked, stomped, elbowed. No bell brought a break in this boxing match without rounds. The men were beaten unceasingly for an hour. By the time the knockout was declared, the five servants were dead.

Chapter 19

Winnie was asked to leave the meeting that evening because she wouldn't stop gabbing about the deaths of the servants that afternoon and everyone she had seen at the square and what they had done. Gabe escorted her to the door and told her she could rejoin the meetings when she learned to hold her tongue. When he shut the inn door behind her, he shuddered at what he had just done. *How did I get the courage to do that?*

The meeting was small that evening. Gabe guessed more than half of their number had been imprisoned, although he wasn't really sure what that number was—he had never counted. Gabe wondered about the men and women missing. *Had they been arrested or did they just switch loyalties, like Marcus and Brad Winsley?*

He had run into Marcus in the square one day. Marcus had taken his hat in his hand and had averted his eyes. He had repeated the same thing he had said at the meeting: he was just doing what was best for his village and his family. After apologizing, he had walked away without ever having looked Gabe in the eyes. Gabe had decided not to go after him.

He wandered around the inn's dining hall, greeting people. He heard one man recount how he had escaped arrest on Sunday. Hearing the happy ending, Gabe repeated to himself, "The King made a way." At one table, he stopped to introduce himself to a young man, a few years his elder.

"Hello." Gabe reached out a hand. The young man took it and returned the greeting.

"My name's Gabe."

"I'm John, and I know who you are." John smiled and pointed at Emily and her husband, sitting across from him at the table. "Those are my parents. You came and helped them out when I was so sick with that virus that went around the village. Now it's just the three of us at home; my brother died then. My parents have been coming around here ever since then I guess, but this is my first time joining them."

"I remember coming to your farmhouse. I was glad to help out." Gabe spied Angela drifting by, watching. He pulled her over and introduced his sister.

John said hello, but Angela just smiled back shyly. Gabe had guessed John was about eighteen, but there was something else he could tell just by looking—he was handsome. Gabe could see that in Angela's eyes.

147

After a time, the meeting fell into its familiar routine: Gabe's impassioned plea and Angela's melodic voice. Even when she read from the King's law, you could hear music in her voice.

Before everyone had emptied the inn, Gabe took John aside. Gabe wondered if in a few years, he would be able to look him straight in the eye, but presently he got an eyeful of Adam's apple. He tilted his head and asked John why he had come to the meeting.

"When Vulpine asked us to kill those men in the square, I knew I couldn't have anything to do with the man. It made me sick. Listening to you talk about the King…it was just the opposite. I know he's someone I can honor."

Gabe was ready with another question. "Tomorrow I'm going to try and visit our friends who were arrested for not attending the singing ceremony. Would you like to come with me?" John shook on it and a new partnership was formed.

Bread and cheese filled two long baskets along with apples Mother had stored in the cellar to preserve during the winter. Angela had tucked a copy of the King's law into the bottom of one of the baskets and covered it with a plain white cloth edged with roses. She thought of the nights she had spent with red thread wrapped around her pointer finger doing the fine work, and she was happy that her labors could serve such a purpose. She admired her cornucopias but knew they would only feed each prisoner a small amount.

"Come home" was all she said as Gabe took up the basket handles.

"The King will make a way." He matched her reticence and was gone.

John was already waiting for him in front of the inn. "Let me help you with that." He took one of the baskets. With the wind chilling their cheeks, they walked the full length of the village: they left King's Hill behind them, passed John's family farm, peered in the shops in the square, skated over a bit of the lake and, for the first time in their lives, walked into the jail.

The guard had opened the door for them without hassle. Inside, another leaned his wooden chair against the wall, warming his hands on a cup of coffee. "What business do you have here?"

"We've brought some food for your prisoners," John answered.

"And for me I hope." The guard's voice was calm and casual, as if they were old friends.

John looked to Gabe.

"Sir, I see you have a warm cup of coffee there and probably had a warm breakfast this morning too. Have your prisoners even had a cold meal today?"

"What do I care about the prisoners?" The guard turned gruff. "Let me see what you have there." The front legs of his chair struck the hard floor. He took his time getting up and walking over to them, boring a hole through Gabe with his stare. He poked through the baskets and said in disgust, "Bird food. But the wife might like this here." He tugged hard and quick on the cloth and yanked it out from under the food spilling a dozen bread rolls onto the floor. "Clean up this mess," he ordered and then laughed.

John and Gabe dropped to the ground and quickly put the rolls back in the basket, thankful the heavy cheese and apples remained in the bottom covering their secret contents. They looked at each other, unsure of what to do next, when the guard helped them out unexpectedly.

"Go and feed the birds. It'll save me the trouble later." He was back in his chair, leaning against the wall and watching the steam rise from his cup.

The boys followed the other guard. The cell door had no window, just another small door through which food could be passed. When the guard was about to open the smaller door, Gabe interrupted.

"We can't really pass a whole basket through that little opening. Couldn't we just take it in to them? I'm sure they haven't been causing you trouble, and if we cause trouble, you could always lock us in there too."

John's eyes widened in disbelief at what Gabe had just said.

The guard just shrugged and opened the larger door. He shut and locked the door behind them. John wondered if he would ever see that door opened again.

"It's me, Gabe."

"Gabe, it's me, Caleb."

"Hi. Hi everyone," Gabe greeted the inmates anonymously in the pitch black room. "I don't even know where you are. I can't see a thing." Gabe elbowed John and covered his nose with his shirt. The prisoners obviously weren't allowed out of the room for any reason.

"My name's John. I've come with Gabe. I'm new to the meetings. We've brought some food." John felt awkward talking to unseen strangers.

Voices came from every angle, greeting, thanking, asking for food.

"I don't know how to get the food passed out. How many are you?" Gabe asked the blackness.

"Forty-two." Caleb seemed to be the leader of the group. "Your eyes will adjust in a bit. There is a tiny bit of light coming from under the door. Not enough, but at least you can tell if someone's right in front of you."

"There's only a small amount for everyone: half a bread roll, a bit of cheese and half an apple. Sorry." Gabe hoped no one would be disappointed.

"Don't be sorry. Sounds like a feast to us," Caleb assured him.

The prisoners organized themselves and came one at a time to get their portion. John handed out the food, and Gabe gave out encouragement.

While they ate, Gabe reminded them of the words of the King's song about his love leading them out of their darkest night. "It will be literally true for you all when you get out of here." Everyone quieted at the comment. "You will get out of here. He will lead you out." He started to sing, and everyone joined in.

"I guess it's time to see if the guard intends to open the door and let us out. I brought a copy of the King's law, but I don't see how you could ever read it in here." Gabe held the precious papers in his hands.

"Leave it with us anyway," Caleb decided. "The King may make a way, right?"

"The King will make a way." The words passed over everyone's lips. Gabe placed the papers into Caleb's hands.

John rapped on the door with his knuckles. All was quiet for a while. "Do you think anyone's going to let us out?" John's voice was unsteady.

"The King always makes a way, John. He always makes a way." Gabe's sure voice gave John confidence, at first.

John took his fist to the door this time. No one spoke. Everyone was waiting to see what would happen.

John bit his lip and tried again—this time knocking continuously. They heard the clang of keys against the metal door. Light flooded in. John thanked the guard. Gabe took a good look at all the faces and saw joy. "We'll try and come tomorrow," he said on his way out of the cell.

"Thank you, sir. We will see you again." Gabe spoke to the guard who was still sitting in his tipped-back chair leaning against the wall. John was pretty sure he was asleep.

Outside John confessed his anxiety. "I thought I was trapped in that reeking black hole forever. How were you so calm? You didn't know we were going to be let out."

Gabe smiled. "I guess I should tell you my story. It started with a toad." Gabe shared with John about all the times he had seen the King make a way. "It's just that…it's just that I know the King. I know him." Gabe shrugged, not knowing how to explain. "When you know him, you just know that he has to make a way. It doesn't mean never being locked in a dark room. But for those people in there, he's made a way for them to be okay. I'm…I don't know how to tell you any better than that." Gabe felt inadequate, but John had understood.

153

"We'll go back tomorrow, right?" John was ready for more.

Gabe hadn't even finished his story when the King had done it again. Before the guard had closed the door, he had asked the prisoners about the song he had heard them singing. "I haven't heard that in years. It kind of brings back memories. If I left the delivery door open, do you think you could sing it again, so I can hear it better?"

"Of course," Caleb said with a smile. Boom. The guard closed the heavy metal door. Clank. He turned the lock. Creak. The little delivery door was opened. Light, enough light to read by, seeped into the cell.

Chapter 20

Gabe and John took Angela with them when they went back to the prison the next day, Friday. The guard let the light shine in through the hatch, and Angela sang for him. They all enjoyed eggs, hard-boiled by John's mother. Several people recited parts of the King's law that had changed their lives in some way.

One woman recited from memory, "Do not let your heart be troubled, and do not be afraid." She told how these words ended her suffering from panic. She explained how she had developed a fear of being inside after the hailstorm had sent the ceiling crashing down around her. She would jump at every noise and constantly look up at the ceiling, nervous it was going to collapse on her again.

"But when I learned those words," she said, continuing her story, "it was as if all I had to do was to say yes to those words, and the fear disappeared. All I had to do was to decide

155

that I would obey those words of the King, and somehow he did the rest. The fear and anxiety were gone."

Gabe, John and Angela left the prison with full hearts. Before they could go back on Saturday, Caleb bounded into the inn, his shaggy hair bouncing along with him. "You're home!" Angela cried out. Gabe came, shook his hand and asked what had happened.

"I don't know. The guard just opened the door and said, 'Go.' We were too excited to ask him why. We just ran. And I didn't stop running until I got here."

"Now what?" Angela wondered out loud. "What's going to happen tomorrow?"

"I don't know." Caleb didn't have the answer. They would know soon enough.

That evening they decided to meet in the middle of the day on Sunday. They didn't like the worrisome feeling of not knowing what was happening to the others. The next day, most were present for the meeting.

They were singing the King's song when the same six guards burst into the inn. They didn't bother with knocking this time. The servants didn't try to run or hide. The head guard looked around and ordered the others each to take one prisoner. Six servants were hauled off in the cage. Caleb escaped arrest this time—John had not.

Monday was a blustery day, and Phineas held his cloak close while addressing the crowd. He announced the reconstruction of the Assembly Hall. He also announced that from that day forward, it was illegal to sing the King's song. The door guard at the prison hadn't heard though—he had been on duty—and John got to serenade him with the others that evening. John also got to enjoy a bowl of warm stew which Angela had made herself. She and Gabe hauled it all the way to the prison on a borrowed cart.

Returning home they were laughing as they walked up to the inn and wondered if it was wrong to have such a good time visiting the prison. Their laughter abruptly stopped when they reached the door and saw a notice had been nailed to it. The inn had been closed to the public, their meetings and their business shut down by order of Vulpine. Again they were unsure of the future, tomorrow even. It was getting to be a familiar feeling.

Mother was furious over Vulpine's edict. "What have I done? What have I done? You are the ones having the meetings. I held my peace about it. Now look what you've all done."

Gabe and Angela stood mutely before their scolding mother. Father still kept to the family quarters upstairs and could not come to their defense. Without interrupting, they let her speak her mind.

157

"What are we going to eat? I ask you. What are we going to do? Spring is around the corner and the inn would finally be getting in some guests and now....What are we going to do?" She put her hand over her mouth and began to cry, her tears watering the seeds of bitterness.

Gabe had a suggestion. "You could take Father's woodwork to the market to sell. It's just like the King had it planned all along. Father's been making them for years now, and you've always complained they are just sitting around. Why don't you try and sell them?"

Mother wouldn't acknowledge that the King had made a way for their family to have another business. She just shrugged her shoulders and said, "Maybe." Gabe smiled at Angela but didn't say another word.

That night, as people showed up for the daily meeting, they were turned away. Many gathered in various homes. Some just returned to their own homes, unsure. Although Gabe and Angela couldn't tell people what would happen to them, there were two things they absolutely knew for sure: the King was alive and he always made a way.

It was on those two points that Gabe spoke at John's house that night. Then John's father spoke with every bit the passion of Gabe.

Gabe and Angela were back to the prison on Tuesday. While everyone ate, Angela told John about Mother's tirade.

He tried to comfort her. "She still loves you. She just doesn't understand. She couldn't possibly understand. The King will make a way for your family to survive. You believe that, right?" Angela nodded and smiled, and to John her smile lit the dark room. When he was released from prison on Saturday, John's first stop was the inn.

Gabe was glad to have his partner back because Angela could no longer go on prison visits. Mother had her working around the inn while she was in the market selling Father's wood carvings. Father continued to spend part of his days whittling but also took some time each day to work on copying the King's law to give out to others. Gabe and Angela didn't have time for that any longer.

The winter daylight was short, but the work days were long for Gabe and John. Tirelessly they spent their days giving out copies of the King's law, teaching other servants and visiting the prison. Each Saturday the jail was emptied, and each Sunday it was filled again. Those arrested were glad there was always a group of them. The body heat of the others was the only thing keeping them from freezing in the bitterly cold cell.

Climbing up King's Hill in the icy cold, the members of the Brothers and Sons grumbled at Vulpine for deciding to meet at Assemblyman Tate's residence just beyond the forest. At the meeting, Vulpine's mood matched the weather.

159

His words were darts with no target to aim at other than those present. Some felt the need to duck.

"I've become king, and here I am still with those who refuse to submit to me." Vulpine spat his words, practically foaming at the mouth. "There is still talk of the previous king living. There is talk of following his law. What are you doing about it?"

Everyone stirred, but no one answered. It was common knowledge that remaining silent was the best response when Vulpine's anger seethed. "I want everyone serving me. We need to end this rebellion permanently." Vulpine paced. Everyone waited for the plan. Vulpine always had a plan.

He stopped his movement and looked piercingly into each pair of eyes. "We need to know who is with us. We need some sort of sign, a mark that would show someone has devoted himself to my service. What can we use?"

Assemblyman Tate suggested a pin that looked like the village banner. Vulpine shook his head. "They could take it off at will and be loyal or disloyal depending on who was present. I want the villagers to be loyal. I want them to be mine." The village doctor cringed at the word "mine."

"What are you thinking then?" Tate posed the question.

"A tattoo: distinct, obvious at a casual glance, permanent." The word permanent landed heavily in the middle of the room.

160

Vulpine turned again to the doctor. "Are you able to help with this?"

The doctor shook his head. "I've never tried it." He paused and then added, "Isn't there another way, a way other than scarring people?"

Vulpine ignored the doctor's question and repeated his instead. "Are you able to help with this?" Vulpine wasn't asking politely. The words squeezed out through clenched teeth.

"I've never done it." The doctor shook his head. "I don't think I can do it."

Vulpine's left eye twitched at the thought of someone saying no to him. For an achingly long moment, he just glared at the doctor. Everyone was tense. Would Vulpine accept no for an answer?

Vulpine broke off his stare and addressed the whole group again. "Who can help us?"

Tate's adult son spoke up. "I know someone who can make tattoos, a cousin of mine. I'm sure that if he were paid for the job, he would be happy for the work." Tate nodded in approval at his son's suggestion.

"Fine. Make arrangements with Phineas for the payment. The design will be a simple letter V tattooed onto the back of the right hand. I expect you all to be first in line." When he spoke, he looked only at the doctor. The doctor kept his head down.

"Phineas will make the announcement this week and will encourage people to take the mark to show their loyalty. Please show favor to those who take the mark. Give them the best service when in your shops. Show them respect. Do the opposite to those who refuse the mark. Leave them standing outside in the cold. Deny them whatever you like. Help people choose their loyalty swiftly. I'm counting on you all."

Vulpine's feet pounded out of the room, and everyone breathed a sigh of relief. The doctor didn't lift his head. He kept looking at that heavy weight which Vulpine had dropped in the middle of the room—permanent.

Chapter 21

Assemblyman Tate and his son were the first to receive their tattoos. Phineas introduced the idea of the mark to the villagers with a great deal of patriotic talk. He urged them to show everyone that they were loyal to the village and to Vulpine by taking the mark. He pointed out that it was free for everyone so the whole village could be united by this simple act. "For peace and unity" was again the explained inspiration behind the mark. No one could argue that peace and unity were not desirable things.

Most of the Brothers and Sons took the mark right away, though a few hesitated. Tate offered some bribes to get other more visible members of the village to take the mark. Tate also took his nephew out to the market stalls and encouraged each seller to take the mark right then in order to prove their loyalty to the others. Gabe's mother was in one of the stalls selling Father's woodcarvings. She looked around at the others and followed them in taking the mark on her right hand.

All of the sellers had taken the mark until they reached the farmers selling their produce. Many of them turned it down. Mother knew why. She shook her head, tsk-tsking them for being so foolish as to listen to her young son instead of listening to the king. She admired the dark V on her hand and was confident she was the wise one.

She showed it off at home. Gabe looked at it with sad eyes but without comment. His mind started thinking through the implications of a mark of loyalty, but he decided he couldn't know what was to come of it. Instead, he refocused his thoughts on serving the King.

Serving the king was exactly what Vulpine determined everyone should do. While having rewarded Tate's efforts to get the villagers marked for their allegiance, he was agitated that the doctor had yet to take the mark himself. He couldn't sleep for want of knowing if his loyalties had changed. One sleepless night, he decided the doctor must be forced to take the mark or take his punishment for abandoning his oath to serve him until death. If the doctor no longer served him, death must swiftly follow.

Vulpine knew his personal appearance in the square would cause quite a stir, so he sent Phineas to complete the assignment—the doctor must be forced to choose. Phineas strolled into the doctor's store front along the edge of the square. "I've come to see the good doctor," he called out in a friendly tone.

The doctor pulled back the curtain to see who had entered and then closed it again to finish tending to his patient. He wasn't in a hurry. He had expected Vulpine to make a move. He knew he couldn't refuse the mark for long without being noticed by Vulpine's eagle eyes, or at least his spies.

He locked the door after his patient left and invited Phineas behind the curtain for a private discussion. The doctor was the first to speak. "I know why you've come, but I'm not taking the mark. I'm not going to be permanently branded for Vulpine. He's only a man." He sighed.

"He's more than just a man now. He's the king, and he can do whatever he likes. And it's your job to *do* whatever he likes." Hearing Phineas talk in that sharp manner reminded the doctor why he had never liked Phineas, but he remained quiet and let Phineas deliver his message. "You made an oath in order to join the Brothers and Sons, and you have enjoyed the privileges of membership. You pledged to give your life to serve Vulpine, King Vulpine. You have only two options here. Fulfill your pledge or lose your life."

Phineas thought the choice obvious, but the doctor didn't respond. He pulled back the curtain and walked over to the front window. Looking out over the square, he reassured himself he was making the right decision. He turned and looked Phineas in the eye. "I can't serve him any longer. I am a doctor, but in serving Vulpine I have used these hands to kill rather than to heal. That's not what I agreed to. I agreed to use my skills to serve Vulpine and, by extension, the village. You know we all thought things would be better if we controlled the village. But now things are worse, and *we* don't control anything. Vulpine just wants to control us. I'm taking myself out of his hands."

"That's not so easy," Phineas retorted.

The doctor looked out the window and watched the villagers passing by. They were ignorant of the decision he had just made. He wondered how many of them had thought through the consequences of taking Vulpine's permanent mark. He smiled faintly at the innocent children chasing each other, bobbing in and out of the crowds.

Suddenly, a man started kicking the door. He was carrying a small boy in his arms. Blood rushed from an open wound in the boy's head. Phineas was the first to the door and used the key to open it. He talked to the man then slammed the door shut and locked it again.

"What are you doing?" The doctor asked Phineas as he approached the door to open it. Phineas blocked his path and held fast to the key.

"What? That man? He isn't marked. He's not loyal to the king and so does not deserve to see the doctor." Phineas' cold-blooded comment sounded every bit as if Vulpine had said it himself.

"I can't do this. I won't serve Vulpine any longer."

Phineas saw that the doctor had made up his mind and shrugged his shoulders.

"What is to happen to me? What has Vulpine said?"

Phineas whistled in response. "I'm not sure he's decided. Neither of us expected you'd actually refuse the mark."

The doctor looked closely at Phineas. "Where is your tattoo?" The doctor's eyes grew cold.

"No one questions my loyalty to the king." Phineas returned the hard look.

"Do you have any loyalty to yourself?" Phineas made no response except to turn the key in the lock and let himself out.

The doctor looked out the open door and noticed Gabe and John walking through the square, carrying baskets of food on their way to the prison. Seeing Gabe with the food basket sent a picture flashing into the doctor's mind of the kind boy who had brought soup during his lowest moment. As if by impulse, he dashed over to them. The sight of the gray-haired man chasing the boys across the square gave many a reason to chuckle, but when he stopped running and the amusement faded, they turned their attention back onto themselves without wondering further what had been the reason for his rush.

Gabe was surprised by the doctor's approach, but he greeted him respectfully. Then, right there by the well in the center of the square, the doctor shared his heart with the boys. "Gabe, right?" Gabe only nodded. "I didn't remember right away when you brought me that soup, but it came to me later who you were. You're not marked, are you?" Gabe shook his head.

"Good. Good. You are a smart boy. I haven't been marked either. I...I don't want to serve Vulpine anymore. I followed him too far, until it cost others their lives. Now, in recompense, I am going to give up my life."

Gabe and John had no idea what the doctor was saying to them, and they especially didn't know why the doctor was saying it to them. They weren't sure the doctor knew why either. They just listened in silence until they saw the desperation in his eyes. Gabe looked deep into the man through those portholes and saw the frantic searching of his heart. Gabe remembered the desperation he had felt before he had met the King.

Gabe reached out and took hold of the doctor's arm and said, "The King says whoever seeks him finds him."

The doctor blinked questioningly and studied the boy's face. The peace he saw there was what he longed for, what he had lacked since signing over his life to Vulpine for a few perks and a feeling of power. "The King? You know the King is alive?" The doctor smiled. "Of course you do. You are the boy from the inn, and the inn had those meetings about the King until Vulpine shut them down."

Gabe was startled that the doctor knew so much.

"You are right," the doctor continued. "The King is alive. I know he is. I know the King's death was faked. I know...I know too many things. Do you still have meetings somewhere?"

Gabe looked at John, who offered an invitation to come to his house for the meeting that night. The doctor looked relieved. They offered to take him to John's house with them after they returned from the prison. The doctor took them up on the offer but made a further request.

"I don't want to wait here." The doctor glanced around nervously. "Could I walk with you? I could wait for you out by the lake."

"Of course you can join us, Doctor. You can stay with us the rest of the afternoon and evening." Gabe's friendly reply comforted the doctor.

As they were walking, the doctor asked one last favor. "Please, just call me Robert. I'm not the village doctor anymore."

The King Will Make a Way

Chapter 22

Robert was obviously nervous, watching over his shoulder and hunching into his cloak. Gabe tried to point out the sun reflecting off the water which shone in the waning afternoon sun, but Robert didn't seem to hear or notice. Gabe whispered to John, asking him to take the food in alone. John nodded and left Gabe and Robert by the lake.

The day was sunny and without wind, though winter's chill still found its way under their skin as they sat watching the light on the still lake. It was too cold for the children to play by its shores now, and the men, young and old, were alone.

Gabe knew the King could relieve Robert of whatever heavy burden he was obviously carrying, so Gabe broke the silence with talk of the King. He talked on his favorite subject, the King's love. Gabe was watching the lake slowly change from silver to gold as he told about the King's ability to take away burdens and didn't even glance toward Robert until he heard him softly say no.

He was shaking his head. "No, you're wrong. There is no love for me. I worked for Hate and Selfishness himself. There is no love for me. I deserve to die, and I will die. No, I don't deserve love."

Gabe wished he knew what Robert was talking about. He was sure that the King could remove any burden, so he told Robert again of the King's great love.

Robert listened intently and wanted to believe him. "Tell me. Tell me everything from the beginning. Tell me everything about the King. I don't have much time. This is my last chance to know."

John walked up to the two and felt like he was interrupting something, even though the two sat for the moment in silence. Looking up at John, Gabe took a deep breath and said, "We should get going before the sun is down." He rose to his feet and helped Robert up. "It all started with a toad."

John laughed to himself, remembering Gabe giving him the same talk in the same place. Robert kept his head down as they walked and instead of acting distracted and agitated, he kept his attention on Gabe's words.

Gabe continued talking with Robert when they reached John's house. The time slipped by and soon Angela had

172

joined them for the evening meeting. John took a seat next to her at the table. Other servants arrived, and Gabe introduced Robert to everyone, though he couldn't bring himself to use his name. He was warmly welcomed by all the servants until Caleb entered and froze at the table's edge.

Gabe stood uneasily when he noticed Caleb's grim expression. "Caleb, why are you here? Is everything okay?" Gabe was wondering why Caleb had left the meeting in his home to come and stare at Robert.

Caleb broke his stare and answered Gabe. "Okay? Thanks to the King everything is okay. But thanks to him," Caleb said and pointed at Robert, who had no idea who this man was, "my youngest son could have died today. Why are you here? Do you even know who I am?" Caleb wasn't yelling, but the usual lightness in his voice had faded to black.

Robert's confusion lifted, and he asked, "Are you the man Phineas refused entrance?" The servants looked at each other with raised eyebrows, asking each other if they knew what had happened. They shrugged their shoulders and shook their heads and waited to see how the drama would unfold.

"That was me. Weren't you there?"

"I was there. I'm sorry he locked you out. I wanted to help. I…I'm sorry. I was too consumed in my troubles to fight Phineas for your sake. Your son's okay?"

Caleb released his frustration and let the King remove its weight. He hung his head.

"I'm sorry too. I am glad to see you here. Are you really here to seek the King?"

Robert's heart leapt with joy. "I am. And I can't believe you are welcoming me here. Then it's really true. Everything Gabe told me about the King is true if you can stand there and forgive me just like that. The boy. Your boy. Tell me what happened."

The servants' hearts rejoiced as they watched Robert welcomed into their number and as they heard Caleb's remarkable tale.

"He's our youngest. He was playing in the barn and fell and cut his head open on a plowshare. He screamed, and I came running to find him bleeding badly from the head. I could see the deep opening in his forehead. I scooped him up and started running. My wife is in prison this week along with my eldest son, but I called out to my other children that I was going to the doctor and would be back. I didn't stop to tell them. I just hollered over my shoulder as I was running past the house.

"My boy stopped screaming, but he looked so scared that it scared me. I got to the doctor's, and it was locked. I just started crazy-like kicking at the door. It opens and who comes out but Phineas. I was startled by that and stepped back instead of trying to just push my way in the open door. He asked me if I was loyal to Vulpine and asked to see my mark. When I had to tell him I didn't have a mark, he said nothing, just slipped back in the door and locked it.

"I was stunned. I was really stunned. I didn't know what to do. My arms were so heavy from carrying my boy, but he looked asleep at that point. So I just headed home, the whole time saying, 'The King will make a way," over and over to myself. Halfway back, I noticed his head wasn't bleeding anymore. When I got home, he still looked asleep. I got a wet rag and wiped away the blood on his forehead. It startled him awake, but I was even more surprised because the wound was gone. There wasn't any cut. There wasn't anything on his forehead."

Everyone was in awe.

"I don't know how, but I know the King did it. He made the way for my son to heal when the doctor didn't." Caleb looked at Robert when he spoke but showed no signs of being upset. "And why did he turn me away for not having Vulpine's mark? Is that a new law?"

Robert was the best qualified to answer. "It's not law yet, but it will be. Right now, certain people have been told to discriminate against those without the mark in order to encourage more people to take it."

"Why do they want people to have the mark? Why is it important?" Caleb asked Robert, who everyone had now realized had a lot more knowledge about what Vulpine was doing than the rest of them.

Robert sighed. "Eventually, everyone will be marked, either by showing their allegiance by wearing the 'V' tattoo, or by showing their disloyalty by not. Then Vulpine can move to rid the village of all traitors."

John saw Angela's face crease with concern. He reached over and laid his hand on top of hers to reassure her. She held her breath until he took his hand away. She let her eyes wander to look at him. His gentle, kind eyes smoothed the lines on her face, but she quickly put her focus back on Robert. John was still looking at Angela when Robert added, "And I will be the first to go."

John turned sharply at the comment to look at Robert. "Why?"

Robert looked weary, his eyes still showing the burden he was carrying. "Let's eat. Maybe later I can answer your question."

Everyone agreed, and Caleb finally returned to his home where other servants were gathered for a meeting.

Robert didn't have much appetite and several around the table noticed he had barely touched his food. No one pushed him to have more. They could all see he was troubled.

176

After the meal, Gabe spoke, as always, about the King's love for the villagers and shared about the King's law of forgiveness. "No matter how many times your friend has to come to you to say he's sorry, you are to forgive him. Think of all the King has forgiven us. We deserve to die according to his law because we all spent years not obeying any of it, but he pardoned each of us when we began following him. He is so merciful and understanding of our failings. As long as we are still seeking him and desiring to live by his law, he will help us to know his law and will help us follow it. If he can do all that for us, we can forgive each other for any wrong."

Robert's heart burned within him at Gabe's words. He had believed him about the King's love, and now forgiveness? Yes, he decided he could believe the King would forgive him, especially as he was prepared to give his life instead of following Vulpine. But he wondered if these people could forgive him? It would be the ultimate test of the truth of their words.

When Gabe finished, he looked at Robert and raised his eyebrows. Robert nodded and stood before the group. "Can you forgive? That's the question I want to ask you. I was asked why I believed I was going to be the first from among you to be killed for not taking the mark. Phineas was in my office today giving me an ultimatum, take the mark or die.

177

He could do that because I am part of a group of villagers who had pledged themselves to serve Vulpine. We have met for years to scheme to place him on the throne. And at his bidding, I have participated in much evil." The shock of the confession sent whispers around the room.

"I couldn't bear his ways any longer and refused the mark. I know Vulpine will see to it that I don't live out the week, if not the day. I know the man well."

Gabe looked around the room trying to catch everyone's eyes and finally spoke for the group. "We forgive you for your part in helping Vulpine. We are so happy you have realized your error and have come to learn about the King. He teaches us to love our enemies, so we welcome you here, though we don't consider you an enemy now."

Gabe had hoped to see light come into the haunted eyes, but they remained darkened. Robert shook his head. "You don't understand what I've done. You don't know or you wouldn't be so quick to forgive, and you could never forget."

Gabe looked at the other servants, all equally unaware of what the doctor was hiding. He sat down and waited for Robert to speak.

"The virus." Robert spoke the words looking straight at Gabe. Again, confused looks shot around the room. The servants shook their heads, not understanding. "The virus that killed close to two hundred people last winter. I created it."

178

The servants still weren't understanding and looked intently at Robert to uncover his meaning. He continued to speak, now with his head down, surprising everyone by his display of weakness.

"Vulpine wanted to create fear in the village so that the villagers would want a leader, a king that they could look to for protection. He asked me if I could create a virus that would spread through the village and kill many in order to create the fear he needed to become king. I had pledged to serve him and unthinkingly unleashed the destroyer on all of you last winter."

In the silence that followed, realization began to dawn among the servants. It was hard for any of them to fathom his story to be true, yet there was no reason to doubt him. Gabe quickly looked around the room. Was anyone angry? Was anyone ready to strike out at Robert?

John's father was the first to speak. "This is my home you've been welcomed into." His voice was calm, betraying no emotion. "Last winter, I lost a son to that virus. He died in this very home. But I still welcome you."

Tears sprang into Robert's eyes as he looked up, disbelieving the grace just offered him.

John saw the good doctor's brokenness and wanted to help in mending it. "I lost a brother to the virus, and I welcome you here with us."

179

John's mother, Emily, spoke quietly. "I lost a son, and I welcome you."

An elderly man spoke. "I lost my wife, and I welcome you."

A young lady spoke. "I lost a friend, and I welcome you."

Each servant took a turn, helping to restore the fragile figure before them. When everyone had spoken, Gabe took the last turn. "You've been forgiven, Robert." Gabe called him by name. Robert looked Gabe in the eyes, and Gabe saw that light had replaced the darkness and peace had replaced the burden. He had found what he had been searching for.

Chapter 23

Gabe and Robert sat alone in the long empty dining hall at the inn. Only one candle burned but gave them enough light to talk together late into the night. Robert mostly kept quiet. He wanted only to listen to the boy with the wisdom and understanding of the King and the humility to know he had no wisdom and understanding of his own.

Gabe obliged and continued sharing about the King. "I don't know if you'll believe me, but you weren't in control of that virus." Robert looked puzzled. "You weren't, and Vulpine wasn't either. The plague was a punishment for the village sent by the King."

Robert's surprised and confused look made Gabe grin. "I don't know how to explain it to you other than the fact that the King is always in control. He somehow always knows what's happening and is in control of the village and what happens to it. It's mind-boggling. I know I don't understand it except to know that it's true. He's proven it true to me thousands of times.

"You thought you were planning in secret and using it all to your own ends, but the King knew about it all and was using it all to his ends. No matter what it looked like."

Robert suddenly burst out laughing. He had to hold his belly he laughed so hard. Tears filled his eyes and he gasped for air. Gabe couldn't help but laugh too at the sight of the sad, worn doctor rolling with laughter. Robert took deep breaths to calm himself, still letting bursts of laughter escape at times.

"Tell me what's so funny. I was laughing at you. You looked pretty hilarious, laughing like a little kid being tickled. What were you laughing at?"

"Vulpine." Robert said with a chuckle.

"I've never found him funny," Gabe said, shaking his head.

"Vulpine thinks he's so smart. He thinks he's five steps ahead of everyone else. And all this time, he's just a part of the King's bigger plan." This time Gabe laughed with Robert, instead of at him.

"It's late, Robert. Stay the night at the inn. We'll see what tomorrow brings. The King always makes a way."

"Thanks for the offer. I would like to stay here with you. And don't worry about me. I know Vulpine won't rest until he's got me, but I'm not scared. Even when he gets his hands on me, I'll know I'm free."

Gabe looked into Robert's eyes; they were bright and clear.

The morning passed peacefully at the inn. Robert looked relaxed. He was sitting in the dining hall with his feet propped up, reading the King's law when the copper bell tolled. He dropped the papers onto the table. Gabe came running into the room.

"Do you know what it's about?" Gabe asked Robert directly.

Robert nodded, stood and used his hands to iron out the wrinkles in his clothes. He calmly put on his cloak and hat and opened the door before he replied. "They're calling me to the Square. I won't keep them waiting." With a nod, he exited the inn.

Gabe ran to fetch Angela. John was waiting for them by the time they left the inn.

"Do you know what's going on?" John looked at Angela, but Gabe answered.

"Robert seemed pretty sure it's about him."

"He still thinks they're going to kill him?" Angela's stomach knotted at the question.

"He hasn't really said much of anything," Gabe explained. "But, he's really changed from yesterday. He was so distraught. Since last night he's really been at peace, even laughed a long time last night."

"Laughed? At what?" Angela wanted to know the joke.

"Vulpine." Gabe started chuckling again, thinking about it. "I'll explain later."

The three teens walked in silence even though the hum of curious villagers surrounded them on all sides. By the time they reached the Square, Robert had already been arrested. He was standing on the Assembly Hall porch with a guard on one side of him and Phineas, greeting the villagers, on the other.

Gabe elbowed his way through the crowd until he was right in front of Robert. Their eyes met, and Robert smiled sincerely. Gabe wouldn't allow himself to be distracted. He wanted to keep his eyes always on Robert so if he needed encouragement, he could find it in Gabe's countenance.

Fellow servants of the King arrived and huddled together in front of the good doctor. Many of them clasped hands, hoping for the best but dreading the worst. The bell finished its welcome, and Phineas spoke.

"Thank you for coming. I know it's a cold day, but we waited for the sun to be its warmest before calling you out." Robert rolled his eyes at Phineas' description of himself as considerate of others. "We were sure that you would want to see justice carried out. King Vulpine, with his vast insight, has uncovered a terrible crime. Never has a crime such as this been committed in our village. It is hard to even speak of. A year ago, a terrible plague descended on our village. Likely more than two hundred people were killed: your fathers, mothers, husbands, wives, your sons and daughters, killed by the devastating virus. It took King Vulpine to lift us up out of our despair."

Robert looked at Gabe. Gabe was relieved that though his face was solemn, his eyes were clear. Phineas gestured toward Robert, who stood straight but not proud. "This man was the cause of that plague. I know it is hard to understand, but it has been proven true. He deliberately made the men training for King Vulpine's guard sick with that virus. It's his fault entirely that your loved ones are dead."

"Give him to us," an angry voice in the crowd shouted up to Phineas. "We'll see that justice is served." The villagers around the man started shouting their agreement and moved toward the platform. Shoving and shouting, their anger festered and the crowd throbbed with violence.

"Justice will be done!" Phineas didn't think more than a few heard him. Phineas gave the guard his orders to take Robert through the square to the platform at the far end and to lock him into one of the wooden frames. The guard hesitated on the first step of the Assembly Hall, seeing the seething crowd. Phineas assured him that they would be more

185

than pleased to let him pass to get his prisoner to his punishment. With a tug at Robert's arm, they started across the Square. They never even made it to the well.

At first, the servants of the King were there to encourage Robert with a word, a pat on the back. Robert had to shout to make himself heard, even to those next to him. "Don't worry about me. I know I'm free!" Gabe felt relief at his words. As Robert stepped out of their reach, Gabe quickly motioned to the other servants to move up and onto the Assembly Hall porch. They all sensed the danger and followed him up the steps.

The crowd pulsated with their hate. The guard shouted at them to give way and resorted to pushing aside those blocking his path. Then someone pushed back. The guard knocked into Robert, causing him to lose his balance. The crowd plunged forward, trying to get at the prisoner, but not even the guard could see him now.

Butting and ramming, the villagers were goats fighting over the single grain dropped in the farm yard. Shouts, grunts and cries emitted from those in the middle of the mass being squeezed in from all sides.

The guard pushed his way out and ran along the edge of the square back to Phineas. "He's gone. My guess is he's trampled under that mob out there." Phineas didn't respond to the report, never even acknowledging the guard. He just looked straight ahead with a satisfied smirk on his face.

"Please Gabe, let's go," Angela begged her brother. He put his arm around her, and they jumped down from the side of the porch, away from the angry mob. The other servants followed. Gabe turned to Caleb and asked him to stay so they would know what had happened. Caleb nodded and remained.

It was a long time before Phineas sensed the crowd had expended its venom and called out for the villagers to quiet, waving his short arms above his head.

"Please, everyone, step back. Please move toward the edges of the square. Let us see what has become of our guilty prisoner." He asked repeatedly until eventually the center of the square lay bare, save for the trampled body of Robert.

Chapter 24

Spring thawed the patches of snow remaining around the village but not the hate that had begun to permeate the hearts of everyone who bore Vulpine's "V"—hate directed at everyone who didn't.

Marked villagers began refusing to sell anything to the servants, the bare backs of their hands showing their disloyalty to Vulpine. Many of the servants were farmers and were thankful they still could provide food for their families and the other servants, but they were no longer allowed to sell their produce in the market.

The servants who had once bought and sold now gave and received. They borrowed from each other freely and offered to each other everything they could spare and some things they couldn't.

When there was a need that couldn't be met among them, there were still plenty of Vulpine loyalists who were willing to make an unfair trade for the item, and one of the servants would find something of value to sacrifice in order to help out their family, as that's what the servants considered each other.

Too many, like Gabe, had flesh and blood family members that mocked or scolded them for their disloyalty to Vulpine. Others, like Caleb, had the joy of living in a home where everyone served the King together.

Although the servants were quick to help and were learning to put each other first, they were still sure the King was helping in many ways as well. One older man with wispy white hair whose cheeks folded over themselves when he smiled loved to tell the others of the time the King had brought his wife dinner. He had been in prison and his wife had been left home alone. One day, she had run out of food but decided to sit down at the table at mealtime just the same. When she went to sit down, she heard a knock at the door. She opened it to find a roast chicken, as plump and savory as she had ever tasted, just sitting there on a platter in front of the door with not a soul in sight. Whenever he told the story, he ended it with a belly laugh and a slap on the thigh.

Some abandoned the meetings for fear of reprisal—they were being bullied, or worse, bloodied. Those servants who remained, grew daily in their understanding of the King's watchful eye and ever caring heart towards them. They also grew in their understanding of the King's law and followed it more closely than ever, always encouraging each other with their stories of failure and restoration as the King had made a way for them.

Gabe's father was always ready to share his story of how he had tried to fight back for the King and had almost lost his life. He never hesitated to share the lesson he learned and to embolden others not to take revenge.

Father had his new conviction tested one day walking home at sunset when it still was cold enough to see your breath. A few teenage boys were skulking behind a stone wall, lying in wait for one of the servants to pass. Father was the unfortunate one to walk past first. A rock pelted him behind his left ear and laughter erupted from behind the stones. Father paused momentarily, putting his hand on the wound. There was blood on his hand when he pulled it away. He kept walking without trying to see who had done it. The boys wanted to get a reaction out of him and weren't going to stop until they had had their thrill. More stones pegged their target, but Father just walked steadily on, not allowing the urge to retaliate to come over him. He had learned his lesson well.

Slowly, it seemed everyone was turning against the servants. The door guard at the jail, when faced with losing his job, took Vulpine's mark. He told Gabe that he was no longer allowed to visit the prisoners, which included Father that week. He also told Gabe and John that the prisoners would not be released until they received Vulpine's mark. Gabe told the other servants the news during the meetings that evening. He played the messenger going from house to house, bringing one more piece of bad news to the weary servants.

John's house was his last destination. He came upon Mrs. Bollix's brother-in-law on his way to the meeting. They walked together until Gabe noticed a "V" blazoned on the back of his right hand. Gabe froze like a deer listening for danger in the woods.

"You have Vulpine's mark," he blurted out, not taking his eyes off the tattoo.

"I had to take it. How was I supposed to carry on with my business if no one would buy from me or sell to me?" the man answered in a defensive tone.

Gabe peeled his eyes off his hand and was speechless at first. He shook his head and said, "The King would have made a way. You can't join us tonight at the meeting."

The man was offended. "This mark doesn't mean I don't serve the King."

Gabe spoke with a firm voice and sorrowful eyes. "Yes, it does. It means you serve Vulpine. You have chosen to serve the wrong king. Only servants of the true King can come to the meetings and gather around the table."

"Who are you to say?" The angry response came, but he didn't try and follow Gabe. He turned around in a huff and walked away.

Gabe let out a deep breath and slipped quietly in the door when he arrived at John's house. He sat down with the others and listened in as they talked about the new developments at the jail. Gabe was thankful John had already delivered the news. He knew the changes at the prison would be a devastating blow to the morale of the servants, and he would much rather bring encouragement.

"How many of you had only the visits and the reading of the King's law to look forward to each day in prison?" asked a teenage boy. "Now they're gone. What will keep them from going crazy in that black pit?"

"They have each other," Emily responded. "They'll encourage each other. Do we know who's in there this week?"

"My wife is in there," said a young man at the table. "When she was arrested, I wasn't even that upset. It wasn't the first time, and we had always been able to count on Saturday releases, even if Sunday they just arrested more. Now, I don't know if I'll ever see my wife again."

Gabe was empathetic. "My father is in prison now too." Then Gabe added his familiar encouragement, "The King will make a way."

John's father spoke to the group at his home that night. He read a portion of the King's law: "The King is a refuge and a shield to those who trust him. He will save them from harm, and they will not fear the terrors of night, the arrow by day, nor pestilence or plague. He will send his punishment on the village, but he will protect those who love him."

John's father laid down his copy of the law and looked at each face before him.

"Do you love the King? He tells us that we love him by obeying the commands he gave us. If you are obeying the commands you know, then you can know you are protected. Do you trust the King? Then you won't let fear into your hearts. It doesn't matter what happens. Vulpine could order us all arrested, or killed. Vulpine could order another sickness from the new doctor. It doesn't matter. Above it all, the King is in control and can save us from harm as the law says.

"I remember John telling me how Gabe first tried to explain these things to him. They had just been to visit the prison. It had been John's first experience of the dark and the smell and the feeling of finality when the door locked shut. Afterwards, Gabe taught John about how the King makes a way for his servants. He said that didn't mean never being arrested. He pointed out how he had seen joy on the faces of the prisoners. The King had made a way for them to be okay. We may want to see it as harm to be arrested, or whatever else we'll have to face, but knowing that the King gives us peace and joy takes the sting out of whatever they can try to do to us.

"Remember that the true harm is what those with Vulpine's mark face every day. Don't you see it? How their hearts are turning to stone? It's like their hearts and minds have been poisoned. That's true harm, and I am thankful I have been saved from it."

Angela smiled at his calm reassurance. John's heart grew full to see her at peace like that. The spring months had gone by in a blur of early mornings and late nights for Angela. As Tabitha grew more proficient at the work around the inn, Angela was able to spend more time helping Gabe and the other servants. She worked from dawn to dusk and in the evenings joined the other servants to gain strength for the next day.

The only break in the routine came at the beginning of summer on a warm June day when Sally Bollix married. Angela, at fifteen, was just a year younger than Sally. Angela didn't join in the festive spirit of the celebration. Feeling pensive, she kept to herself. Standing alone and watching the ceremony with its music and dancing, flowers and laughter, she thought of John. She had heard his mother make a comment or two about Angela turning sixteen in the coming winter. She was thinking Angela and John would marry. Angela watched Sally's groom take her away and pondered what she would have to give up if she had a groom come and take her away.

The days flashed by seemingly without beginning or end. No more arrests were made. Vulpine just left the pressure on those remaining in the prison to take the mark or rot in the dank jail. The rest of the servants had the heavy burden of living in a place where each day, someone new turned against them.

Over the winter, Gabe and Angela celebrated their sixteenth birthdays together. In the spring, John spent a week helping Mother with repairs around the inn since Father was still in prison indefinitely. Mother told Angela that John was "a fine man." Angela couldn't keep her face from flushing at the mention of his name. Yet from time to time, Angela would look at him and ponder the same question, *What would I have to give up if I let him take me away?*

Chapter 25

Gabe lay on the floor exhausted. It was too hot to move anyway. Angela was prone on her bed, blubbering, her pillow soggy with tears.

"I didn't think it would be so hard to say no, Gabe. I was so sure. But the look on his face...I don't think he'll ever want to see me again." She wiped her scarlet nose.

"John will understand." Gabe tried in vain to console her. "Just give him time. He just hadn't realized your commitment to the King. He's committed too. He'll understand."

That morning John had told Angela that he loved her and asked her to marry him. Now he was pacing along a row of corn behind their family's home, wondering where he had missed the mark. So many nights he had sat awake in the dark prison, thinking about that moment and Angela's joyful response. He had had lots of time to think about it; he had been in prison often. It seemed only Angela and Gabe managed to avoid it. But he had been lying to himself. All of his daydreams were just that – dreams. He ripped off part of a stalk.

Gabe felt helpless. Whenever someone was in trouble, he would say, "The King will make a way." He believed it fully, and he used the line often. Now it didn't seem like those words could mend these two broken hearts, two hearts he dearly loved.

Angela sniffled. "Gabe, could you talk to him? Check on him for me. See if he's okay. Explain to him again for me."

Gabe didn't answer right away. He was thinking he'd rather visit Vulpine than go on this mission. *I'd rather jump in the lake in winter. I'd rather live out on the roof for a week. I'd rather eat a slug.* Gabe let out a little laugh before he caught himself and pretended his throat needed clearing. "I'll go tonight when it's cooler outside," Gabe answered. *And when John is cooler.*

That evening Angela went to the meeting at Caleb's house. Gabe went alone to John's. He purposely showed up late so he wouldn't have to talk to John, not yet at least. John's father spoke to the group. He lived the King's words, and they flowed out of him with little effort.

When he finished his message, Winnie stood up. In his preoccupation with John and Angela, Gabe hadn't noticed her. She looked each person in the eye. "I need to say I'm sorry to everyone. I used to come and talk foolishly with you all. I talked too much and told too much and cared too much about what everyone was doing. Basically, I was a gossip. I haven't been to meetings for a long while, but I have been reading the King's law. He has hard words for people like me. Well, hopefully, people like I was. I think I have learned my lesson." With a smile, she added, "And I'd like to thank Gabe for kicking me out of your meetings and sending me home until I learned it."

The group seemed as if they were waiting for Gabe to make a response. He was bowled over by her openness and her courage to keep seeking the King on her own, and he stood up and told her so. "And welcome home. You're part of our family again."

Everyone was on their feet. The women hugged her and kissed her cheeks. It was a thrill for everyone to see this happy ending after having seen others leave the meetings never to return.

After the meeting, Gabe lingered as the others left. John knew he was there to talk to him and eventually made it easy. "Do you want to come see the corn?"

Gabe saw through the offer and acted eager to see the crop's progress. The two walked out past the barn and hopped over the fence rail into the field with only the sound of the crickets accompanying them. John halted on the other

198

side of the fence and leaned against it. He reached down, plucked a tall piece of grass and started ripping it into little pieces.

"It's been a bad day," John started. Gabe had been hoping John would do all the talking. "I've been driving myself crazy thinking about the past year, more than a year, every moment I've ever spent with her. I know it was all the King's work she was doing. I know she wasn't doing it to be with me but maybe some of the time, I was doing it to be with her." He stopped fidgeting and looked at Gabe. "That's what I've realized today, going over everything over and over in my head. I realized that I wasn't only serving the King. I was also serving myself by wanting to be with your sister." He rubbed his forehead.

Gabe realized John wasn't going to say anything else, and he was going to have to think of something to say. He scanned the night sky and took in the stars. Something came to him. "Well, I guess the question is now, do you want to serve the King even if it means never being with Angela?" Gabe bit his lip.

John didn't turn to look at Gabe; he set his gaze over the horizon and spoke into the hazy night sky. "King, I've never met you, but I know you are out there. Gabe says that somehow you know everything, so know this: I choose to serve you until I die, whether tomorrow or a hundred years

199

from now. I love Angela and will always love her as another one of your servants, but I give her up to serve you. In fact, I want to be like her and give up my own life to serve you all the way."

He understands. The King did make a way.

"I want to go tell Angela I understand her decision. Let's go to the inn."

The night was warm but a relief from the baking sun. Angela was looking out the window when she saw them in the distance. She pulled on a shawl to cover her bare arms and leaned out the window, resting her elbows on the window sill. Her eyes met John's as he approached, and she knew from their warmth everything was okay. "I'll be right down," she called to him and withdrew from the window. She walked down the stairs one at a time, taking a breath with each step. She wanted to look calm when she walked out the door. She had been anything but calm all day.

John thought the first frost would nip before Angela managed to get outside. He hung his head and decided she must have changed her mind and didn't want to see him.

"Gabe, I'm going to—"

"Hi, John." Angela cut off his exit.

"Angela." At first, that was all he could say. Looking at her with the full moon reflected in her eyes, he almost forgot, just for a moment, his confession to the King.

Gabe came to the rescue. "John really understands, Angela. He wants to tell you."

John snapped to from Angela's mesmerizing eyes. "Yes, I do. I understand why you said no. And I've told the King." He stopped and smiled. Angela smiled back but raised her eyebrows. This time he avoided being drawn in by her shining eyes. "I did. I told the King that I wanted to be like you and commit myself completely to his service."

Angela held onto Gabe's arm, trying to draw on his strength by osmosis. It would take strength not to think about her past with John or the 'what ifs' of the future. "That's really wonderful, John." She looked at Gabe while she spoke. She could feel the calm slipping away.

She looked up at John and smiled. His heart skipped a beat when he saw her tear-filled eyes. Now it was his turn to feel weak.

Angela pressed the corners of her eyes with her finger to stop the tears from spilling. She looked away and said, "Mrs. Bollix brought over some food for us to deliver to Widow Jenkins tomorrow. I think I'll go get it packed up so it's ready." She braved one more glance at John and whispered, "Goodnight, John."

Angela hurried inside and John swallowed hard, unable to speak. He slowly walked home and made one last trip to the corn field. He sighed heavily and spoke to the corn. "If this was supposed to be one of the best days of my life, what's tomorrow going to be like?"

Chapter 26

"We're not deterring them. Their numbers remain steady. Maybe we've encouraged some to defect, but it's not enough!" Vulpine railed at Phineas and Writ, who stood at attention before the throne. "Have you seen these?" He grabbed a page of the King's law and crumpled it in his hand. His eyes were fixed on the paper and flared red hot. He contorted his face like the thing was putrid and dropped it like it was diseased.

"We've tried to control them through their money." He spoke calmly now, his eyes fixed. "We've tried imprisonment, even death. Those bishops," he snarled, "are loyal to the wrong king, and I won't stand for it."

He blinked and the life came back to his eyes. He scanned the men before him and steadied his focus on General Writ. "Send your men in as spies. You saved some loyal guards to remain without the mark, right?" The General gave a crisp nod.

"Have them find the meetings under the pretense of wanting to be a follower of that ancient man. They are to watch the meetings carefully and arrest the leaders. They are to be taken to the Square. We'll have ourselves a bonfire." Vulpine turned his attention to Phineas and nodded, setting him to action as if he had wound up his mechanical doll.

The servants were in action too. In the morning, John made his way to the inn to meet Gabe and Angela. Together they traversed the length of the village to Widow Jenkins' house. Angela worked on cleaning the house while John made some repairs. Gabe sat by her side and read to her from the King's law.

"Thank you," she said to the three before they left. "I know my old body won't last much longer, but I am thankful I lived long enough to hear those words and experience your kindness. Thank you." Angela gave her a warm embrace before they left. She felt satisfied and wished the good feeling would remain.

Before heading home, they stopped by the lake to cool off. Splashing the water and laughing, the teens felt as free as children again. It was in this brightened moment that John had the impulse to try again to visit the prisoners. The jail was in sight but a distance away. Gabe and Angela agreed, with a flicker of hope that they might get the chance to see Father after a year and a half.

They chased each other along the bank of the lake and stumbled into each other as they reached the prison door. The guard who had at one time wanted to hear the King's song was standing in front of the door.

Angela decided to ask the question. "Sir, do you think you could allow us, just this once, to visit with the prisoners?"

The guard looked forward and unblinkingly responded, "There are no prisoners."

"My father's in there," Angela countered.

"There are no prisoners," the unflinching guard repeated.

Gabe tried. "Our father was arrested two winters ago. We know he hasn't been released. There were at least a dozen others with him." The guard didn't answer.

Angela started to softly sing the King's song. Quickly the guard turned to her. "Be silent. Your father and fourteen other prisoners were executed for refusing Vulpine's mark. Their heads were chopped off and their bodies buried in a heap behind the prison. Now go from here quickly and don't return."

But they didn't move at all. Their feet had turned leaden and their minds lost their direction. Angela suddenly felt like maybe she was dreaming, but a sharp "Go" from the guard made her bolt like a frightened kitten, just wanting to run to the nearest place to hide. She found it at the well and sat propped up against it, with her arms wrapped tightly around her knees. She buried her tear-streaked face in her arms.

The boys chased after her and slid down the well wall along with her, and sat on the dirt, dry and dusty from the scorching summer sun. No one spoke, but their thoughts were racing, tripping over each other, piling up like in a race when the lead runner goes down. The doubts, the fears, the unknowns, the realities came at them with a feverish pace. They were helpless, unable to just dig in their heels and make it all stop before it ended in tragedy.

As if to confirm every dark suspicion of what was to come, across the square, they spotted a large metal cage, three times the size Caleb's had been. Two horses pulled the unsteady cart while four of Vulpine's guards walked alongside, balancing the cage. When they reached the platform, the guards took axes to it and to the wooden frames as well, reducing it all to kindling. With great strain, the guards placed the bottomless cage over the pile of wood, its metal bars striping the sky beyond them. Satisfied with their job, the guards left, leading the horses and cart behind them.

John, Gabe and Angela stared at the oversized cage, its bars a web built to hold its prey. They moved toward it haltingly, like in a nightmare when you want to run but somehow you can only move slowly.

"How many people do you think they expect to round up in there?" Angela wished she hadn't spoken.

"Let's not talk about it," Gabe replied with sadness in his voice. "Let's be about the King's business." His eyes grew steady and his posture more confident.

Not a minute had passed when the bell resounded. "Now what's going on?" Angela's stomach was starting to feel like Gabe's at Vulpine's unveiling.

They found a shady place to sit and waited for the rest of the villagers to gather. The sun was high, promising another sweltering day. The three teens sat together in silence. Gabe once opened his mouth but shut it again without uttering a sound. John dozed off, physically and emotionally exhausted. Phineas' raised voice woke him.

"My friends," Phineas opened his arms to the awaiting crowd, "we have called you out this morning for an important reason. We need your help again. Traitors to the crown have been on the prowl. There are rumors of another attempt on Vulpine's life." Some in the audience gasped. John quickly turned to Gabe and mouthed, "Have you heard anything?" Gabe shook his head and formed a rounded "No" with his lips.

"I know it is the utmost concern of all our good and upright citizens to maintain the peace and unity of our village. These rascals want to steal these treasures from us.

207

We won't let them, will we?" Deep huts and huzzahs bellowed out from the pits of the men's bellies.

"Once again we ask your help. Anyone refusing to attend the singing ceremony is a rebel! Tell us where the rebels meet. Also, his royal majesty King Vulpine has forbidden the production and distribution of literature. These thieving scoundrels have been spreading lies about our wise and noble king with their papers. Please gather any of these papers you find and throw them in there." He pointed directly to the cage in the Square. "Tonight we'll have a bonfire to celebrate our victory over these inferior weaklings who dare to consider standing up to our powerful king."

The majority cheered as victors. The remainder, though scattered, spoke with one small voice in that moment. "The King will make a way."

John, Angela and Gabe set off at a hectic pace. They stopped to talk with all of the servants, encouraging them to remember the King. They went from house to house, talked across fence rails, walked arm in arm. Everyone they could get a hold of they did, and their message was always the same—the King will make a way.

At the same time, other villagers were giving names and locations to Vulpine's guards, reporting on family members and neighbors. Mother was among them.

At the evening meeting, Gabe finally shared the news of the prisoners' execution. The servants rallied around the newly widowed and fatherless. There were tears and laughter. There was a new man in attendance that was discomforted by the sight of their love and joy in the midst of pain and loss.

He listened as different servants shared lessons they had learned from the lives of those who had remained loyal to the King to their death. Gabe was proud that his father's testimony of learning not to pay back evil with evil had had such an impact on others.

After the meeting, Gabe shook hands with the new man in attendance and welcomed him. He just shook Gabe's hand, gave a nod and left. Gabe asked John if he knew who he was and where he had come from. John didn't have a clue.

The man, Todd, shuffled down the dirt path. He had followed orders and found the meeting, but it wasn't anything like he expected. There was no plotting to overturn Vulpine. It sounded like they wouldn't swat a fly if it landed on their noses. He couldn't figure out who the leader had been. They all had spoken in turn.

On the road ahead, he saw his colleagues escorting bound prisoners down the road. No one was fighting. He broke into a jog and caught up with a guard leading John's father from Caleb's home.

"Need any help?" Todd was eager to look like he was accomplishing something.

"Help? Does it look like it? Where's your man?"

"I couldn't make out a leader."

The other guard laughed. "Did you forget our orders? Make an arrest. They want bodies. Don't show yourself to the General without one."

Like a cat pouncing, reality hit. He remembered the "do or die" way the order had been given. He had been sent to arrest the leader and had left without making an arrest. He became resolute that he couldn't lose his job, or his head, no matter how nice these people were. Running back to the house, he saw Gabe and Angela walking home but decided he'd have to get someone who lived at the meeting house in order to be confident that he had someone worthwhile.

Breaking into a sprint, he tore up the path and with full force banged in through the front door, not stopping until he had shoved John to the ground. With a heavy boot pinning John to the floor, he bound John's hands behind his back.

He hoisted John to his feet. "Are you taking me to the prison?" John asked stoically.

"No," Todd said coolly. "I'm taking you to the Square." He broke out in a nervous laugh, knowing John didn't comprehend what was about to happen. As he led his captive out the door, he told him, "You're going to the bonfire."

210

Chapter 27

"Father!" John shouted across the confusion. John was in the square with Todd firmly holding his left arm. His father's eyes searched until they found their target—his son. His heart stopped. He gasped and gave himself a shake to pull himself together. The guard thought he was trying to escape and struck his stomach. His breath left him. Again he gasped and this time, in stillness, garnered the fortitude to face his son.

Todd stopped in front of the cage, and John stood next to his father. "This thing is what I told you about earlier." John had to use his chin to point to the menacing cage that loomed behind them. "Do you know what's going on?" John watched one of the guards throw copies of the King's law into the cage.

His father hadn't answered and John kept talking. "So, that's what this bonfire is about? They're burning all our copies of the King's law. Don't they know we'll just make more? Why the big show?"

Todd moved to face John. "Listen, the bonfire is for you. They don't need bars to hold the papers, do they?"

John's face scrunched in a quizzical expression. He turned to his father who was looking straight at him with a deadly serious expression. Realization dawned. For the longest moment, they just stared at each other. They weren't blank stares, though. They were expressing to each other a lifetime's worth of 'I love you' and 'I'm proud of you.'

"Like father, like son, right?" John tried to laugh off the knowledge of his fate.

Gabe and Angela came running across the square. Another one of the servants had rushed to the inn to tell them what was happening. They headed straight for John.

Catching her breath, Angela started bombarding John with questions. "How did you end up here? What's going on? What are they going to do to you?"

"I was arrested after you left. Go home now, Angela. I'll be okay. The King will make a way."

Gabe learned from John's father what was going on at the bonfire that night, and he told Angela. Shocked, she looked up at John and saw in his eyes that he knew the truth too. "John—"

"Angela, no. It's okay. I told the King yesterday I was going to serve him until I died. I'm going to keep my promise. I'm at his service, and tomorrow you'll serve him

212

just as today." John's voice was solid, and his eyes showed more concern for Angela than for himself.

Angela tried to speak as she held back her tears. John didn't need to hear it; he could see it in her eyes. She finally managed to whisper, "I love you." John took a step toward her but was jerked back by Todd.

Gabe put his arm around Angela and started to lead her away from the scene. With a final glance back at John, Angela was escorted part way across the square. Gabe found a friend to walk with her back to the inn and returned to the cage. He wanted to be there to ensure there would be an honest account of what took place. He spoke to each of the seven men, bound and lined up in front of the dark enclosure, praising them for their bravery, assuring them that their sacrifice was worth the cost and encouraging them to remember the King in their last moments.

One of guards shooed him away like a pesky puppy sniffing at his heels. Gabe retreated into the shadows of the shops. He wanted to run away and hide but determined to stand his ground.

Music began playing. *How can you celebrate such an event?* Gabe felt queasy. Phineas took his place beside the cage, and shouted out to the gathering, "Bring all the illegal papers you found to help us light the bonfire!"

213

A line formed, an ever-shifting centipede, a hundred legs taking little steps forward, bringing copies of the King's law. Everyone took part, children asking their parents if they could be the ones to throw the papers onto the pile. Phineas congratulated them on their successful efforts to end the illegal distribution.

The seven men started quoting the King's law out loud. Neither the guards, nor those tossing in the papers, recognized their words. With each phrase, peace filled their hearts and minds and strengthened their resolve to face the hour with dignity.

Then one woman heard their words and pointing accusingly, shouted to Phineas, "Those are the filthy words! They are saying what's on these papers!" Phineas turned to General Writ who issued the orders for the cage to be opened and the prisoners thrown in. Phineas couldn't risk word getting back to Vulpine that he had allowed the King's law to be taught at the bonfire!

Two guards leaned over and lifted the front wall of the cage. The hinges screamed with the movement. No one fought their escort as the guards shoved them into their final prison. With a screech, the door was released. It crashed closed, and the heavy bang reverberated back and forth across the square before being swallowed up by the night.

"Light the fire!" Writ's order sent shivers down Gabe's spine. He looked at his feet. A torch was thrown into the cage which easily sent the papers into a blaze. Some in the crowd were yelling, urging the flames on, when a soulful note sounded. Gabe knew instantly what was happening. John had begun to sing the King's song. At first, the others suffering the heat didn't join in the song, such was the power of those first notes.

Then John looked to his father; he joined in and the others followed. The seven men with deep, full voices sang of their love for the King and the King's love for them. A woman watching the inferno rage slipped the papers she held into her blouse, grateful Phineas had stopped her before she had abetted this crime. She felt the power of the words and wanted to know them for herself. She excused herself and hurried home, dragging her four-year-old by the wrist.

The men crumbled to the floor of the cage, hidden in the golden glow of the flames; their song was finished.

Gabe took a detour on his way back to the inn. Thinking of John, he jumped the fence lining his family's corn field. It was incomprehensible to think only yesterday he had stood here speaking with John. Following John's example, uninhibited, he spoke to the King.

"Where were you tonight? Where are you ever? Where have you gone?" All the long days, the beatings, the deaths,

215

the imprisonments, the closures, the secrecy, the bonfire; any of it and all of it finally overwhelmed him in that moment of questioning. He roared into the night sky and tears raced each other from both corners of his eyes. They slipped and sledded down his cheeks, streaking his face and dripping steadily off his chin. He ignored it all; his focus was on the King.

"You promised to come back to us down here one day. I know you are coming. Why not now? Why not tonight? What are you doing? Why are you letting all this happen? I want to talk with you! I love your words, your law, but I love you too, and I want to see you again! I want to be at your feet!"

His gut was twisted in knots. He flopped down in the grass and rolled onto his back, spent. He gazed into the starry night sky and started to doze off. He startled himself awake with a jerk of his limbs. Calmed, he struck up his conversation again.

"I'm sorry, King. I know I will see you again. You made the way for me to see you in the first place. You will make a way again. And you made a way tonight for those men. They weren't afraid. Somehow you kept them at peace. They didn't cry out in pain. They sang your song. You made a way. You always make a way."

216

THE KING WILL MAKE A WAY

Chapter 28

The homes where the seven men had been arrested were boarded up in the morning. The inn bustled again as Caleb's family and John's mother, Emily, moved in. Caleb's sons helped Emily with her farm and both families helped supply the inn. Having guests at the inn should have brought the color back to Mother's cheeks, but bitterness had left her pale and drawn. Her love had grown cold; now scorn marked her face.

Tabitha was growing into her mother's image daily. Now a young lady of eleven, she was a constant helper to Mother in Angela and Gabe's absences. She mirrored her mother in more than looks. She parroted her thoughts on the King.

More copies of the King's law were made and given to those who had lost theirs in the raid. There wasn't much reaching out to tell others about the King's law any more. The village seemed entirely segregated—them versus us. No one knew where it would all lead.

Over the winter, Gabe and Angela didn't celebrate when their seventeenth birthdays passed on a drab, gray day. Another sweep of arrests were made, and the servants tried not to think the worst. The only light in the dreary winter months was the servants' sweet time of fellowship which seemed to stretch longer each day.

Daily they felt the weight of their persecution. Spring came but didn't lighten the load. It wasn't until the oppressive heat of summer pressed in on them that much of the other oppression suddenly lifted.

"The King will make a way," parodied Vulpine from his throne. "The King is dead!" he bawled, heaving himself forward as if to throw his words over the trees and into the valley below. Leaning back and looking disgusted he added, "Didn't anyone tell you?"

General Writ had just given his status report and looked agitated by Vulpine's state. Vulpine gripped the arms of the throne. "I'm waging a war against an enemy who doesn't fight back, and I can't even win. How is that possible?" He growled the question.

Writ knew better than to answer. He remained at attention and let Vulpine go on his verbal rampage. "We need to find the one." Vulpine held up one long finger. "We need to find the one who had the first copy of that outdated law book. Learn where it all began, and then take out the backbone of the operation. Stop the arrests. Let up for a while so they'll feel more open. Then find him."

Writ understood the last command was not optional. It would be his life or that backbone. He had to find it and break it. He started by calling off all sweeps of homes by the guards. The guards were told to keep away from any meetings and to stop any harassment of the servants that they witnessed. They even released the prisoners from the jail. The extremely thin but joyfully alive prisoners returned to their families.

Relief swept through the meetings. The worst was over. The King had kept his word and brought them out of their darkest night. They no longer had that anxious feeling that they were about to get some horrendous news. Everything seemed better—the air fresher, the sky bluer, their steps bouncier.

Maybe it was this free feeling that kept Emily from seeing anything wrong with listening to Mother speak of Gabe's visits to the King in the market place. Squeezing vegetables, stroking fabric, bartering prices, they weaved their way through the stalls. Mother was talking about her children and how much things had changed once Gabe had started climbing King's Hill daily.

They came to the well and rested their bodies and their bags against it. "He said he was visiting with the King." She looked at Emily a bit sarcastically. "You know which King I'm talking about. He would wake up while it was dark, even in summer when the sun's up earlier than the roosters, and would be gone a few hours every day.

"He rarely said anything at all for a long time. I guess none of us listened to him, except Angela. She has always loved that boy. But now all these people listen to him. Even if I think he teaches some fool ideas, I'm still kind of proud of him."

She chuckled, thinking of Gabe as a young boy. "When he was a wee thing, he wouldn't even say hello to people. He was six before he would reply to a friendly greeting. It's the truth. Now look at him, talking at your meetings." Her eyes and her voice dropped. "But what good is his having confidence if it just gets people killed." Emily had no reply.

They hadn't noticed that the woman drawing water from the well continued to do so until their conversation had ended and then had left without taking any water with her. Hoisting their bags to begin the walk home, they were completely unaware of the part they had just played in Vulpine's plan.

"A boy?" Vulpine repeated incredulously.

"Yes, Your Majesty, a boy." General Writ was pleased to serve Vulpine the information he had desired. "And not just any boy. Do you remember Gabe from when we had our meetings at the inn?" Vulpine searched his memory and found a mop-haired boy, who had never spoken a word or looked a soul in the eye for all the time they had used the inn for their meetings.

"Gabe?" The surprise still hadn't left Vulpine's voice.

"Yes, sir. He was only ten when he started visiting the King, and he hasn't seen nor heard from him since he disappeared, and you took the throne."

Vulpine sat higher than the morning sun, which was making its daily morning climb as Gabe had done for three and a half years. At ease, Vulpine lounged in the throne and ruminated on the information. Moments passed before a wry smile cracked his face.

Abruptly, he jumped to his feet, as excited as a school boy just promised his own horse. "This will all be finished soon, General, my brilliant General, who brought me this delectable delicacy today." Vulpine was intoxicated with the assured final victory over this defiant enemy.

"Let's bide our time, a few weeks—just before the harvest. Until then, watch the boy. Learn his daily routine. Know where he goes. We need to be able to find him when the time comes. Don't let him escape. Set your guards around the perimeter of the village watching for an escape attempt.

"I will question the boy myself at a trial. When he fails before the entire village, the whole of it will crumble with him. He'll be hung for treason." Cackling, Vulpine slid back into his seat. He finished his chortling with a happy sigh.

The King Will Make a Way

Chapter 29

With the exception of Mother and Tabitha not joining in their meetings, everything seemed just about perfect. So it came like a bolt of lightning on a clear summer night when the door guard from the prison brought news to the inn early one morning.

"You're to be arrested." The guard made no other introduction and looked directly at Gabe as he spoke.

"What?" Gabe didn't comprehend what had just happened.

"I can't stay. I wanted to warn you. I remembered your kindness and well..." He stopped and looked over his shoulder nervously. "I have to go, but just know they're preparing a special cell for you. They're going to arrest you after dark, tonight. I need to go." In a flash, the lightning faded, but the dark storm clouds remained.

Gabe's family surrounded him and sat him down with them at a table. Caleb's family and Emily huddled around. All at once, everyone started talking.

"We can sneak you out of the village this afternoon."

"We can hide you in the cellar."

"If we can get you over to our place, no one is checking the boarded up homes anymore."

Gabe started shaking his head, slightly at first and then more vigorously until he vocalized its message. "No!" Everyone backed off at his firmness. "Let me stand, please." Gabe's mother moved and let her son out from the bench. She sat and looked up at her son.

"For seven years, I've been escaping." He spoke to the floor as he paced back and forth. "I didn't run away. The King just…" He stopped pacing and smiled at his audience. "The King just made a way. So, if he's not making a way for me to avoid arrest this time, he must be making some other kind of way. Look, we've all known this was probably going to happen someday. They must have finally realized who I was. I'm sure most of the time they didn't pay attention to me because I was a child." Gabe stood as tall and straight as a soldier at attention. "Now I'm as tall as Father ever was and can't hide anymore. I won't hide."

He leaned on the table. "I'm not saying I'm looking forward to whatever is going to happen tonight, but I'm not

224

scared either, and I don't want you to be. And I'm thinking, if I'm going to be arrested anyway, I might as well do something worthwhile to get arrested for. I don't want to be arrested just sitting at home."

Gabe pushed himself back from the table. "I'm going to go speak about the King in the Square. Maybe I can convince some new people about the King before they finish my special cell."

No one argued with him. They knew he wouldn't back down from his plan. Mother set her jaw, slid out from the table, tugged at her apron and said evenly, "Before you go, you'll need a big meal." Emily followed her into the kitchen.

Caleb helped Gabe gather up all the copies of the King's law, leaving just the one original copy in the inn. He planned on giving out all he could. Caleb rejoined the family and Gabe sat alone with the King's words. He had turned to them time and time again in order to prepare for whatever lay ahead. Knowing at least a sliver of what was to come, he consumed those words again to gain the strength and wisdom he would need.

Angela was sent to fetch Gabe to eat. She peeked in the door to the family's quarters to find her brother in a familiar posture, bent over those tattered papers. She thought it amazing they hadn't disintegrated with use. She dreaded pulling him away from this comfortable scene. She had lost

John and Father; her stomach was churning just thinking about not wanting to think about what might happen to Gabe.

"Gabe," she called to distract herself, "Mother has your food ready. She's expecting you to come now. She and Emily made so much you might not be able to stand afterwards."

Angela laughed but thought maybe Mother was thinking the same thing and making a desperate shot at keeping him home. Gabe didn't mind the reasons behind it; he just enjoyed the food. Whole eggs, rolls laced with cinnamon, cheese and meat slices, apples with sugar. He feasted like it was his last meal, thinking maybe it was.

When the last crumb was eaten and every last finger licked, there was nothing left to do but say goodbye. Gabe wanted to march straight out the door, but he dutifully hugged and shook hands with everyone at the inn—Caleb's family first, then his own. Mother's tears were a mixture of sadness and anger. Tabitha hugged him quickly, and while Angela's arms were wrapped around him, she whispered to him one more time, "The King will make a way."

He strode out of the inn without looking back. He made straight for the Square without knowing exactly what he was going to do when he got there.

He stepped into the openness of the square. It was abuzz with activity. He started strolling along the shops and saw a weaver busy at his trade, sitting at his loom, weaving threads into cloth with a steady clapping of wood and the smooth slide of the shuttle back and forth.

Gabe walked past the glassblower, who had garnered an audience. He was blowing the glass up like a balloon. When his onlookers were sufficiently awed, he pricked the balloon. Pop! The light reflected off a hundred flecks of glass being carried by the wind like the seeds of a dandelion. Gabe reached out a finger to catch one as it fluttered by.

The light breeze gently encouraged Gabe forward. He left the shelter of the shops at the edge of the square and crossed towards the well in the center. Gabe let a laugh escape as he remembered calling it the Square's belly button when he was little. He looked around quickly to see if anyone had been watching.

The ground was wet around the well, a sure sign of fall. He debated climbing onto the wall of the well to speak, but remembering his mishap and the dark chill of the well water, he chose to remain on the ground.

He took a deep breath and plunged in. "There is only one King who rules our village," he shouted over the clamor in the Square. "Vulpine is the imposter. He has lied to you, to me, to the whole village. The one true King is alive! I have seen him and met with him. I will tell you about him."

At first, people scurried away from him, embarrassed to be standing by the shouting young man. Others further back

227

stopped to listen. Their ears were ringing with the foreign words of love and a living King. Some laughed, thinking him crazy, while others were drawn in by his passion—either way they gathered to listen.

He told them of his days at the feet of the King. He told them that the King would return to rule and that they would be sorry if they weren't found on the side of the King. He told them of the King's laws and quoted them by heart. The words of the King were burned on his mind and filled his heart until they poured out from him wherever he was.

He didn't need to think about what he was saying. The words flowed past his lips as easily as a river passes over a pebble and they flowed with as much power as a river cascading over a waterfall. Tears filled the eyes of a woman standing several feet from Gabe; she was holding the hand of her five-year-old son. She recognized the words from the papers she had tucked away the night of the bonfire. She called out, interrupting him, "Have you really seen him?"

Gabe dammed the current. He stepped forward to speak directly to the woman. "I've seen him. For three-and-a-half years, I met with him daily. I sat at his feet and learned from him and was loved by him." She searched his eyes and found a treasure of love and truth.

"I believe you."

A man standing next to her, having heard and seen the encounter, asked loud enough for everyone to hear, "If we believe this is all true, what can we do?"

Gabe reflected as he walked back to his post by the well. "If you believe, then there is only one thing you must do. You must give yourself entirely to serving the King and obeying his laws. The King must be your first and only and everything. You must be prepared to give up your home, your family, your belongings, your last breath in order to serve him alone."

The man was shaken by the answer, but the woman walked up to him and stood in the mud by the well. "I'm willing." She slipped her son's hand into her sister's. Several stepped back and faded away. One reported to a guard what was being said at the well.

The guard hurried to break up those congregating by the water. He knew he could lose his head if he allowed this kind of chatter under his guard. When he saw the copies of the King's law, he grew frantic. He knew he couldn't let those get out of the Square. He ordered everyone to throw their copies into the well then asked who had broken the law by distributing them. Gabe turned himself in.

The woman chased after Gabe and the guard. The head prison guard recognized Gabe and told his captor of the big fish he had just reeled in. Then he asked about the woman.

She spoke for herself. "I deserve to be arrested. I am no longer loyal to Vulpine."

The guards all looked at each other. Spotting her marked right hand, the head guard said, "I can help you with that," and walked out of the prison.

The others waited in wondering silence. Gabe grimaced when he saw the guard return with a hatchet. "Put your hand on the table." The woman hesitated for just a moment then placed her hand on the table and pinched her eyes shut. The hatchet came down heavy and wedged into the wooden table. The woman pulled her arm away without her right hand.

"Thank you," she said calmly but stared at her arm, unmoving. Gabe started to pull off his shirt, and the guard released him so he could wrap it around the woman's wound. She smiled at him and walked out of the prison. Free.

The King Will Make a Way

Chapter 30

When Gabe was alone with his captors, they stripped him and shut him into the cell, which was more like an indentation in the wall. There was no window or even a little delivery door. Apparently, no one expected to be feeding him.

There was no room to sit, so Gabe would be forced to stand all day and all night. He leaned has bare back against the wall, closed his eyes and sang. When he finished, he started again. Then he worked on reciting the King's law word for word, starting with page one. He had read it so many times he could just about do it. The song and the words had the same effect. He was experiencing his darkest night, but he was at peace. Despair no longer hunted him, stealthily encircling him, waiting for a weak moment in which to pounce. Despair had no home there with him. In its place there was hope.

Mother, on the other hand, had no hope or peace. When she felt she couldn't stand the torment of not knowing any longer, she sent Angela to the Square to see what was happening. Angela sped out the door as fast as a falcon swoops towards its prey.

Stopping to catch her breath in the southeast corner of the square, she noticed a gathering at the well and went over to investigate. It wasn't hard to discover what had happened. Everyone was talking about Gabe and the King.

Gabe's river of words had spilled its banks. More and more people had gathered around the well. The guard returned from the prison and threatened them with arrest if they didn't disperse. They slowly edged away. But the guard had just created tributaries, each person a rivulet meandering through the Square leaving sedimentary news that the King might be alive.

Angela didn't speak to anyone. She felt detached from the scene, floating from pair to pair, listening in on the chatter. Angela's feet touched the ground right in front of the Assembly Hall where her eyes transfixed on General Writ. He was standing on the porch of the Hall listening to the reports of two guards. One told of arresting Gabe, the other of talk that the King was alive.

Writ was noticeably flustered by the intelligence he had received. "Bring me a horse!" he barked at no one in particular, but a horse was promptly provided. Angela stood in the settling dust watching the galloping horse trace its way to King's Hill and wondered what response the news would bring.

"He's altered the plan!" Vulpine was irked by the revelation. "The arrest was to be made in secret tonight. He was to be kept in his cell without food or drink or sleep for two days before we announced his arrest and trial to the public. I want him weakened for that trial!" Vulpine realized what he had just admitted in front of the General and quickly recanted.

"Never mind. All the better. Let's be done with him and the whole thing. We need to stop the spread of those vicious rumors he started. Send Phineas to announce his arrest and to warn people of his harmful, scandalous talk. He's to announce that the trial will be in the morning." General Writ gave a curt nod and set off.

Vulpine spoke to himself. "He's already weak. He's a boy. He never even went to school. I am a learned man. He can't cope with my wisdom. He will fall before me, and I will prove to everyone Lord Vulpine is the king!"

Hooves frantically drumming the road was not an everyday sound in the village. Caleb opened the door to see who was racing past the inn, not once, but twice that afternoon. Smiling, he noted to those gathered that Gabe had

Writ dashing madly about, trying to fix whatever damage had been done by his speaking in the Square.

The dust was flying again, and Angela backed out of the way of the speeding equestrian. She lurked in the shadows of the Assembly Hall on a reconnaissance mission to discover her brother's fate. She scouted General Writ recovering his composure after his frenetic race to the Square. He disappeared into the Assembly Hall and reappeared with Phineas, who gestured to the villagers in the Square.

"I'm calling on every man and woman to be in attendance for a trial in the Square tomorrow morning. Our protectors have succeeded in capturing a dangerous criminal who has been spreading vicious rumors. King Vulpine himself will question the liar and expose his lies. Our village will not tolerate anyone sowing seeds of disunity. Do not believe his lies or spread them further. King Vulpine will lead us all to the truth!"

Angela hurried home with the report. The inn, though full of familiar sights and smells, felt odd and empty without Gabe. The families quickly gathered around Angela, and she shared all the details she knew.

Caleb took off to spread word of the trial. Other servants began filtering into the inn, feeling the need to be together at the loss of Gabe, who up until that day had seemed

234

untouchable. For the first time in more than three years, they sang the King's song all together in the inn.

Hours went by and the candles were lit, no one wanting to leave the inn or the feeling of strength that comes with numbers. Mother, however, went up to the family quarters with Tabitha, as usual, while the meeting was still going on.

Angela went to sleep reluctantly that night, not wanting the comfort of fellowship to end and to have to face the long, dark, unknown of the night alone. She dreamed she and Gabe were down in the Square, watching them build those wooden frames. Whack. Thwack. Tap. Tap. Tap. She stirred from her sleep. Her eyes shot open wide. Whack. Thwack. Tap. Tap. Tap. The hammering echoed through the village, sending another code. But what was its message?

She raced alone to the Square. She didn't need an explanation of what she was seeing this time. There was a new wooden platform next to the Assembly Hall with a tall neck. From its bowed head swung a hangman's noose. The gallows. She swallowed hard. She made a hasty retreat like a roach when a candle is suddenly lit. She felt exposed and wanted to hide. She wanted to bury herself in her bed under pillows and covers as she did as a child to feel safe from a thunderstorm. But she knew this was a storm she'd have to face.

The King Will Make a Way

Chapter 31

The servants were sober in the morning as they made the journey together from the inn to the Square. The bell rang out its welcome, inviting everyone to the event. The whole village was turning out—mothers with still swaddled babies, old men barely moving with canes, the merchants, the farmers. Everyone with eyes and ears wanted to be in the square to see and hear Vulpine and his foe.

The bell's ring slowed, sounding more and more distant as Gabe was brought nearer and nearer to the Assembly Hall. Vulpine had ordered him dressed in a plain night shirt that hung to his calves. His feet were bare, and his wrists bound behind him. One of Vulpine's personal guards led him on a leash, like an untamed animal needing to be reined in.

Gabe walked without struggling. His head was up and his eyes were steady. A full day without any nourishment or sleep had accomplished an unexpected result in Gabe; he was steeled to prove the truth about the King.

Gabe's leash was tied to a pillar on the Assembly Hall porch. His fellow servants amassed just in front of him and could see the calmness in his eyes. Angela and Gabe locked their eyes on each other and neither blinked as Vulpine was announced. Angela moved her lips to form the familiar phrase, "The King will make a way." Gabe knew it was true—he just didn't know if that meant release or peace at his execution.

Two guards opened the door to the Assembly Hall. With all royal pomp and pride, Vulpine stepped forward onto the porch. With a scepter in his raised right hand, he greeted his subjects.

"Thank you for your presence at this trial. We need your help in order to end, once and for all, the lies being spread by this weasely scoundrel. You, my beloved subjects, will act as jury. You will do your duty to denounce his lies and to order his treachery ended by means of the gallows!"

Cheers erupted from around the Square. Silence was present as well in the circle of servants before Gabe and in a one-handed woman clinging to her five-year-old son.

Vulpine spun on his heels to face Gabe, his robe twisting behind him. "Do you plead guilty to the charge brought against you yesterday at the time of your arrest; namely, the unlawful distribution of literature in the village?"

"I do," Gabe answered evenly.

"Please repeat your answer again. Are you guilty or not guilty?" Vulpine was exceedingly pleased with himself and his immediate victory in the trial.

"Guilty." Gabe spoke in the same even manner.

"Let everyone in the jury know that the defendant, Gabriel, has pleaded guilty." Vulpine walked to the edge of the porch and egged on the crowd. "Am I not being proved correct that this is a scoundrel that should be done away with?" Vulpine relished the yells and cheers of the villagers.

"Now let's turn to a more serious matter. You have been spreading vicious lies around the village. The most serious lie is that the previous King is still alive. Have you spoken this lie to anyone in the village?"

Gabe caught Vulpine's crafty words. "I have not lied," Gabe called out, his voice stronger, "but I have told many people that the true King is still alive." A muffled cheer came from the small circle in the crowd in front of him. The servants may have been outnumbered, but to Gabe, that dot was like the North Star in a sky cluttered with constellations—all that was needed to lead him home.

Vulpine didn't back down. "So you admit you've spoken this outrageous falsehood numerous times. A lie, I may point out, which amounts to treason."

Gabe didn't respond but kept his eyes on the North Star to steer him straight.

"This trial will then quickly come to a close, for from what you have openly admitted your only recourse is to prove this King is alive. I leave it in your hands. Can you prove it?" Vulpine was gleeful.

Gabe pierced the expectant silence. "I have seen the King!" The fullness of his lungs and diaphragm supported the words and carried them to the edges of the crowd. The words were met by gasps and guffaws. Vulpine quickly intervened.

"Another lie! You can't keep wielding your slippery tongue without evidence. If you say the King is alive because you have seen him, then again I say to you, where is the proof? Show us the evidence that you have seen him." Vulpine's eyes narrowed into slits, arrow slits made for one purpose only, to destroy the enemy.

The North Star seemed to dim. In all the years they had listened to Gabe speak of the King, he had never offered evidence that the King was alive. They each had felt it for themselves, but how could it be proven?

Gabe searched the sky again for the words as he had done his last night with John. Instead of finding a solution, he spotted a star. A new star seemingly had appeared in the sky, bright enough to be seen by day. Gabe squinted and tilted his head back trying to get a better look.

Villagers started to follow his stare. They began pointing and whispering. The blood was rising in Vulpine's face at having lost the momentum and focus of the trial. He brought everyone back to attention, shouting, "The defendant must provide evidence of having seen the King or be hung!"

The solution came. Gabe addressed his jury. "After it was announced that the King had died, a beautifully carved cabinet was brought to be kept in the Assembly Hall. Where did that cabinet come from?"

"The King's throne room." Everyone knew the answer. A chorus of voices responded, a cacophony of sound.

"It came from the throne room of the previous King, who is still the true King of the village."

Vulpine burst again in his rage, "Where is your proof?"

Gabe remained as steady as a cat on its feet and continued his conversation with the jury. "And what was the one thing that was kept in that cabinet?"

"A plate," the crowd answered eagerly, enjoying the game they were playing.

"Not any plate but a plate made out of solid pearl and trimmed in gold, the plate of a King."

Vulpine had regained control of himself and now just rolled his eyes at Gabe's antics. "Having had a cabinet and a plate does not prove the man alive nor that you have seen him." A few chortled along with Vulpine.

Gabe ignored the interruption. Angela was beside herself. She was the only one in a thousand who knew what Gabe was doing. Her stomach flip flopped. She didn't think she could bear the suspense of waiting to see the outcome. It was a horse race and her stallion had just come from behind and was pulling into the lead. Don't trip now!

"The first time I visited the King on the hill, he showed me that plate and told me it was my invitation to sup with him whenever I wanted. I request that the plate be removed from its shelf where it's been since the fire and shown to the jury as evidence."

Knowing the whole village had shuffled past that plate time and time again to inspect it, Vulpine waved his fingers at a guard to bring it out. Waiting for the guard, Gabe again spied the golden star in the sky which seemed to have grown larger. He gaped at it along with half of the villagers.

Bellowing again, Vulpine restored everyone's attention to the proceedings. He didn't like Gabe speaking so much and wanted to draw this to an end as soon as possible.

The guard had brought out the plate. Gabe looked at the plate expectantly, but with his hands tied behind his back, he couldn't touch it. His name had been there seven years ago. It had to still be there, right? He wondered if the fire could have seared off the writing. His hesitancy made Angela's heart skip a beat. Taking a deep breath, she called out, "The King

241

has made a way." She quickly shrank into the crowd as guards advanced toward her, but the damage had been done. Gabe had regained his footing.

"I ask that a member of the jury be permitted to join us on the porch to examine the evidence." Gabe was again as confident as a lion ruling his pride.

Vulpine was leery. "As villagers, the guards are part of your jury. I permit this guard here holding the plate to observe it for the jury at large."

Todd, the guard, nodded at Gabe. He remembered the last time he had seen him, just before pushing John into the bonfire cage. He gave Gabe a questioning look.

Gabe eyed the seemingly approaching star and somehow drew on its energy. He lifted his voice and called out, "Please clearly tell your fellow jury members what is the only word written on the back of my invitation to visit the King."

Vulpine shuddered and went pale. Todd carefully turned the costly plate over to reveal its underside. There was only one word there. "Gabriel!" Todd shouted it loud and clear.

The crowd erupted at Gabe's name and so did Vulpine. He grabbed the plate and smashed it to the ground, sending fragments in every direction. He grabbed Todd fiercely by the throat as if by shouting alone he wouldn't get his orders across. "Hang him!"

Todd was shaken, but fear of Vulpine's wrath spurred him to move quickly. He untied Gabe and dragged him stumbling to the gallows. He slipped the noose around his neck while the crowd screamed and roared.

Vulpine stormed across the porch to knock Gabe off and cause him to swing to his death. As his heavy boots thundered their way to Gabe, an even louder sound split the scene.

An earthquake violently shook the Square. The terrified villagers were knocked to the ground and tossed about. The Assembly Hall split from its foundation and, toppling backwards, was shredded by the trees behind it. The whole square reeled. Crashes came from around the square as shops creaked and cracked and threw their stock. The long neck of the gallows snapped in two. Gabe slipped himself free from its grasp and stood steady on its platform. Vulpine was flung off the Assembly Hall porch, which splintered. The other servants of the King were still right in front of the remains of the Hall when the earth ripped in two and a sinkhole opened on the far side of the Square, swallowing hundreds of villagers, who disappeared under the earth before most had any idea what was happening.

When the tremors lessened and the stunned villagers regained their bearings, they began to stand to survey the damage. What they saw knocked them right back to the ground. The star had disappeared from the sky, and not only was Gabe dressed in brilliant white, but beside Gabe on the platform stood the King.

THE KING WILL MAKE A WAY

Chapter 32

"The king is dead!" Phineas had scrambled over to Vulpine, lying prone on the ground. Seeing his chest still, he had made his final announcement to the village. He eyed the King and slunk away. Heading toward the hill, Phineas froze in front of the inn when he saw a few dozen people all dressed in white approaching him. When he recognized Robert, the good doctor, among them, his heart stopped and he collapsed in the road. They walked past his body on their way toward the Square, while the birds rejoiced above them.

In the Square, the villagers were on their knees before the King, more majestic in appearance and presence than they could have imagined possible. Vulpine, in comparison, had been a slug.

The servants, all now clothed in white, bowed in awe. Without a word from the King, the other villagers remained bowed to the ground and began weeping in guilt and fear. At the same time, a nightingale began to sing. A skylark alighted on the broken neck of the gallows and warbled. A dove perched on the platform and cooed. More birds began circling in the blue sky, adding their voices.

Angela was the first to pick it out. She recognized the birds' song—it was the song of the King. She stood, a lone tree on the savannah, and sang with the birds. The servants began to cry tears of their own. Years of terror had broken them, and the beauty of Angela's voice and the lyrics of love washed their wounds. By the song's end, they had been made whole.

Angela began the song again, and this time all of the servants stood and sang the King's song. With one voice they praised the King, *His love a banner waving over all of us, a beacon leading us out of our darkest night.*

The King had made a way.

Made in the USA
San Bernardino, CA
23 July 2014